THE TREASURE, THE DICTATOR AND THE SPY

JAMES WOODWARD

1

Lisbon, Portugal
May 1939

The night was the sort of dark that only occurs during rainstorms along the coasts of oceans...wet, howling wind, bitter cold and inky blackness. The driving raindrops tasted salty. The only dry places were indoors next to roaring fires. But Isaak Baumel was not indoors. He was wrapped in a long wool coat, stomping his feet to keep some semblance of warmth circulating through his body and waiting for his contact. He wasn't unhappy to be alone in this place...it had been crowds and their insanity that had sent him.

Out of the darkness loomed a figure even taller than himself, also wrapped in a long wool coat. A black knit seaman's cap was pulled low over the man's ears. He came close to Isaak and spoke Polish in low tones. "No nightingales, tonight."

"They've all flown south," Isaak answered.

There was no need for such code words. As soon as one man heard the accent of the other, he knew he was authentic, but it couldn't hurt.

"Dr. Baumel?"

"Yes."

"Congratulations. You've made it this far and you're wise to get out of Poland. Even now, the Nazis are on the move. You came all the way by train?"

"With my wife and two daughters. We had many close calls and anxious moments, but we're all safely here."

"You have the money?"

"I do. My wife pawned her jewelry in Madrid. They were the only things of value we were able to bring with us. We left our home, our furnishings, our art, and our comfortable lives...but, I think we're the lucky ones. Is there a ship that can take us to America?"

"The British ship we'd planned for you to go on, leaves in two days."

"Planned?" Isaak's heart sank. "What do you mean? Is there a problem?" Had they come all this way only to have their hopes dashed at the last moment?

"You can still go on her if you want. No one will stop you from getting on board. But the German U-boat captains are eager to begin sinking British ships. When the Germans invade Poland, England will have no choice but to declare war on Germany and it won't take long for things to spiral out of control."

"U-boats? What are U-boats?"

The tall man gestured to the other side of the harbor. "Three of them are moored to the quay, over there. Can you see them? They hunt in packs beneath the surface of the sea. You don't know they're there until torpedoes slam into the hull of your ship and blow it out of the water."

Isaak squinted into the rain. Across the water, he could make out three, sinister, black shapes slunk low in the steel-gray water that lapped around them. He shivered. "They couldn't look more evil."

"You're right about that, Baumel. So, what do you think? Do you want to go?"

"I don't know. I'd be playing Russian roulette with my family's lives. What about Morocco? It's close to here, isn't it? I know people who've gone there. Is that a possibility?"

"Not really, the Germans have established a presence there, too. However, there is one other option, if you can leave tonight. A Spanish boat's leaving for Cuba at midnight. The captain says he 'll take you for the same price as the British boat."

"Cuba? What's Cuba?"

"It's an island in the Caribbean Sea, near America. They speak Spanish there. It should be a safe passage. When war breaks out, Spain and Portugal will remain neutral. The U-boats won't fire on a Spanish vessel."

Isaak looked back across the water at the three German submarines and pondered his decision. A blast of cold, wet wind struck him in the face. He turned his back to it and faced the tall man. "It's good that the ship leaves tonight...my youngest daughter isn't well. It's been a long hard journey and I want them out of harm's way as quickly as possible. We're ready to go. We'll be back at midnight."

"Good."

Isaak paid for their passage and the two men shook hands. Then, Isaak walked back through the rainy night to tell his family of the new plan. The heaviness had lifted. The air was still cold and wet and tasted like salt, but it smelled of freedom.

2

The steel handrails of the pitching ship were cold and dripping wet. It had become his habit when he came on deck to search the seas for any sign of the deadly U-boats. But tonight, the bitter wind and stinging rain caused Isaak to hide his face. He held tight to the handrails as he climbed.

"Ah, Dr. Baumel," the captain said when Isaak entered the pilot house. The captain spoke only Spanish, but Isaak was learning.

"*Buenos noches*," Isaak replied.

The captain laughed. "You're picking up the language quickly, Baumel. What kind of doctor are you?"

"I was a psychiatrist in Poland."

"Ah, a doctor of the mind. I'm sure I would benefit from your services." The captain laughed, again.

Isaak smiled. This response was common among the lay people to whom he revealed his profession. "I want to learn to speak Spanish well and I want my daughters to learn and become real Cubans."

"No problem for them...they're beautiful girls. They'll be very popular in Cuba."

"Thank you, Captain. Yes, and I hope the warm climate will be good for the health of my youngest daughter...she's been coughing since we left Poland. I'm also thinking of changing their names to something typical in Cuba. Could you advise me on this?"

"A name is an important thing. I'm honored that you consult me."

"My eldest daughter is called Juljana in Polish. What do you think?"

Like seamen everywhere with time on their hands, the captain enjoyed considering possibilities. He snipped the ends of two cigars, lit Isaak's and then his own. He leaned back in his chair and lifted his feet onto the ship's dashboard. He watched the blue smoke from his cigar swirl above him, as though he might find the answer there. "I think maybe Juliana," he said at last. "Yes, Juliana would be fine. And the younger one?"

"Her name is Olga."

"That one is simple, the name is the same in Spanish. She can remain Olga. It's a common name in Spanish."

Isaak was surprised but pleased with the simplicity of the solution. "Juliana and Olga. Thank you, Captain. Excellent."

"I've been all over the world," the captain said. "People are not so different."

Isaak nodded in agreement. "No, they are not so different."

The men sat back, smoked their cigars and reflected on the truth of the captain's statement. Soon, however, Isaak's mind returned to the fear that had gripped him since they'd left Lisbon...the ghostly German submarines lurking somewhere in the depths below. They weren't *supposed* to fire on a Spanish vessel, but mistakes could be made. The voyage could take several weeks...plenty of time for someone to do something stupid. Isaak shuddered. The boat groaned with the force of its exertions, the sea washed over its decks and the rain continued.

It was a few days more until the storm finally abated. The family awoke to sunny skies and calm seas. Juliana rose first but soon came running back to their stateroom. "Come quickly," she cried. "You must see!"

They hurried to join her at the rail. As the morning mist dissipated, a large island revealed itself before them. Green mountains rose from the blue sea. White, puffy clouds drifted lazily across a blue sky. Juliana leaned against her father and hugged him at the waist. "It's so beautiful," she murmured. "Now we'll be safe, won't we, Papa?"

Isaak smiled and hugged her in return. "Yes, my child. Now we'll be safe."

3

Santa Fe, Cuba
June 1946

A line of brown pelicans coasted imperturbable along the ridge line that separated the mainland from the beach, their necks nestled between their shoulder blades. They rode the updraft of the warm Caribbean breeze that rippled across the sea and created twinkling diamonds on the water's surface. Violetta Valiente looked out past the laundry she was hanging and imagined, as she had so many times before, what it might be like to walk across the water and pick up those diamonds. Further out, a flock of snowy-white egrets wheeled en masse, pure and clean against the backdrop of a bright-blue morning sky.

"*Mira, Mami, mira!*" Violetta's attention was drawn from her laundry basket and clothesline to her barefoot children who were running up the slope of the beach. Behind them trudged Violetta's younger brother, Tomo. His body was that of a pudgy, full-grown man, but his mind had not kept pace. Affable, but slow-witted, Tomo raised one arm above his head and waved something he was carrying in a signal of triumph.

Violetta surveyed the sky. Plump, white clouds were beginning to form. They'd grow taller throughout the day and by late afternoon it would rain very hard for a little while, but the clothes would be dry by then and folded safely inside the house.

She smiled to see her children racing to her across the yard. Her insides ached when they were away from her and seeing them made her feel whole again. Maria's long black hair streamed out behind her as she ran, lustrous in the tropical sun. Roberto was struggling hard to stay in front—his short legs churned in quick, furious steps. Tomo was trying to hurry—half running, half stumbling. Violetta had sent him out with the children two hours ago to net shrimp at the mouth of the Taoro river. Poor old Tomo, what did he have, now? First Roberto and then Maria ran into her arms, both talking at once.

"Pipe," Roberto gasped.

"River…cross," Maria said.

"Calm down and catch your breaths," Violetta said. "I can't understand what you're saying." The children danced around her and pointed to their uncle who clambered up the slope on all fours and waddled across the grass. In his right hand he clutched their find. Out of breath, he stretched out his arm to Violetta as a gesture of self-explanation.

Violetta looked down at the dripping object in his hand. It was cylindrical and, perhaps, twenty centimeters in length. Its actual girth was difficult to estimate due to the sedimentation that caked its surface. Whatever it was, it looked like it had been in the water for a very long time. "What is it?"

"We don't know, Mami," Roberto said. "We ran back to ask you. We were shrimping and I felt something hard down in the mud."

"Tomo pulled it out and washed the sand off it," Maria said. "Some of the crusty stuff came off, too. That's when we saw the cross."

"The cross?"

"Yes, Mami," Maria said. "Show her the cross, Uncle Tomo."

Tomo turned the object over. "*Dios mio*!" Violetta put one hand to her mouth and crossed herself with the other.

"That's what we said, Mami," Maria said. "So, we ran home to show you."

Violetta reached out and touched the cross with one finger. "It's the sign of the holy savior."

"What should we do, Mami?" Maria said.

Violetta shook her head, her face lost in wonder. "I don't know…we must wait until Papi gets home. He'll know what to do."

4

Ernesto Valiente lined up the soft wrapping leaf with the tightly rolled and pressed tobacco and cinched it with the first turn of his fingers. Then, in one swift motion, he pushed his palm across the table and rolled the rest of the wrapping leaf around the inner tobacco. He licked the last bit of the wrap to hold it tight, put a dab of glue on one end and sealed it with another lick of his tongue and a turn of his fingers. Each new cigar was his next masterpiece.

How long had he been doing this? Twenty years? He never grew tired of it. He was a large man…over six feet and 200 pounds, but his fingers could work delicate magic. Whenever Winston Churchill placed an order for his beloved *Figurados*, Ernesto was appointed to do the honors. He was proud when he saw the picture of Churchill with Roosevelt and Stalin on the front page of the Havana newspaper. The world leaders were meeting at Yalta to plan the defeat of Hitler and jutting from the mouth of Churchill was one of *his* cigars! That called for a stop after work at *La Bodeguita* for a few *Polars*. Of course, almost every day called for a stop on his way home at *La Bodeguita* for a few *Polars*, but that time had been special. His money was no good that day. Everyone bought his beers for him, slapped him on the back, called him by his nickname, "Macho," and told him how important his cigars were to the thinking processes of Churchill and the fate of the world.

Ernesto smiled, as he started the cinch on another wrapper, thinking about his family—his wife, Violetta, his oldest child, Maria, and his son, Roberto, whom he called his little "Machito." He rolled his palm across the wrapping table again. "You're a lucky man, Ernesto…a very lucky man," he told himself. He stopped thinking about himself and his good fortune to listen to the Lector who sat on a small stage at the front of the cigar factory. They'd voted this week to listen to Ernest Hemingway's *For Whom the Bell Tolls*. Ernesto had read it before, himself, and the reader was just getting to his favorite part—the part where Robert Jordan and the girl made love—the part about the frightened rabbits and the earth moving. Thinking about that made him smile some more.

Ernesto stopped at *La Bodeguita* after work, but only stayed for a couple of beers. "Cubilete, Ernesto?" someone called from across the bar. The invitation was accompanied by the sound of dice being tumbled inside a leather cup.

"No," he said. "I feel lucky, but I'm going home."

The sky was streaked with orange…the color of ripe tangerines. The heat of the day was retreating, shadows were lengthening, and the breeze was cool. Ernesto carried his lunch pail and whistled to himself as he walked through the dusty, scrub palmetto, down the winding road of sand that led to his house. When he came in sight, the children began calling, "Papi! Papi!" and ran up the road to meet him. Barefooted Machito reached him first and leaped into his arms.

"We found a pipe, Papi! It's on the table in the kitchen! We put newspaper under it!"

Ernesto looked at his son and smiled. "What are you saying, Machito? You make no sense."

Maria reached him next. Ernesto held Machito in one arm and put the other around her shoulders. She skipped and hopped beside him. He was only able to get "pipe," "cross" and "river" from her. He shook his head—he'd have to get the real story from Violetta. She was coming now, walking slowly, and swinging her hips. Her pretty mouth and eyes smiled at him with their secret. She couldn't wait to tell him, but she wanted him to be curious about something she knew that he didn't. Tomo beamed beside her.

"What is it, Mamí?" Ernesto said. "What is it that has you all acting so crazy?"

Ernesto sat at the kitchen table to view the marvel from the river's mouth. He continued to hold Machito in one arm while he studied the cylinder. The rest of the family huddled close around him. After a few moments, he reached out with his free hand to touch a crusty side of the object…more flakes fell away. "It looks like it's made of lead." He grasped it in his hand and hefted it. "Heavy, yes, I think it's lead." He turned the pipe to one side so he could look at the marking of the cross. "I've seen this type of cross before," he said. "I've seen it in the drawings and paintings of the ships of Christopher Columbus. Their sails had this *estampa* on them. It was the symbol of the Spanish King, Ferdinand, and his Queen, Isabella."

"*Dios mio*," Violetta said. "Columbus?"

"Well, no, this is probably not from Columbus," Ernesto said. "Columbus did land in Cuba in 1492, but I don't think he came this far up the coast. But later, other Spanish ships did land here when they were bringing their treasures back from Mexico and South America. They called Cuba, the 'Queen of the Antilles'. It was their last stop in the New World before they returned to Spain."

"But what is it?" Violetta said.

Ernesto laid the pipe back on the table. "I don't know, but it must be very old."

"What should we do with it?"

Ernesto shrugged. "I must think about this. Is dinner ready?"

"*Sí*," Papi, I have had *ropa vieja* cooking all day."

"Then let's eat and I will think."

They ate and Maria told the story, again, of how they'd found the pipe. Tomo nodded in agreement with her statements. He watched Ernesto's face for signs of what emotion he should be displaying. Ernesto looked serious, so Tomo tried to look serious, too.

"We were casting the net for shrimp, Papi," Maria said. "Roberto stepped on something hard."

"It was low tide?"

"*Sí, Papi,*" Tomo said. "It was low tide!"

"Yes," Maria said. "I think the tide was just beginning to turn, Papi."

"And where *exactly* were you?"

"On the riverbank," Maria said, "near the beach."

"The Taoro?"

"*Sí*, Papi, the Taoro."

Roberto listened to his sister's story and watched his father think. He watched his father's hands steer his fork through his food. The muscles in the sides of his jaw tensed and relaxed when he chewed. But mostly, he watched his father's eyes. They were soft and dark with heavy brows, and they stared at the cross on the side of the pipe. This was the most exciting time Roberto could remember. He was filled with wondering what his father would do.

"Should we take it to the authorities?" Violetta said. "It must be valuable."

"You're right, my little heaven," Ernesto said. "This could be *very* valuable, which is exactly why we should *not* take it to the authorities—tell me one of them that you think you can trust."

Violetta sighed and shook her head. Ernesto was right, she could think of no one.

"*Sí*," Ernesto said, "there is no one. If we take this to *El Cuartel*, the *sargento* there will confiscate it, and *no one* will ever see it again." Then Roberto saw his father's face change. He pushed his empty plate away and sat back in his chair. "Machito?" he said, not taking his eyes from the pipe.

"*Sí*, Papi."

"Go to the closet where I keep my tools and bring me my metal saw…the one with the little teeth…and some oil, *por favor.*"

Roberto ran to the tool closet. He returned with the saw and put it on the table in front of his father, along with a hemispherical brass can. A tube jutted from its top.

Ernesto patted him on the head. "*Gracias*, Machito," he said. "Now we'll see if there's something inside this pipe."

Ernesto held the pipe with his left hand and began to saw just inside the end cap. As he sawed, he turned the pipe. When he'd finished one complete rotation, much of the deposit had flaked off. He continued to move the saw back and forth across the pipe. Lead filings sprinkled onto the newspaper with each stroke. He made a small groove in the lead all the way around the pipe.

The family watched as he worked. It was a little saw, but he was making progress. The groove deepened and began to bind on the saw until Ernesto could no longer move it back and forth through the metal. He turned the can upside down and pressed its bottom several times, as he turned the pipe. The can made a metallic popping noise when he pressed its bottom and oil squirted into the groove he'd made. "Now, we can do better," he said. The filings mixed with the oil and came off in a black sludge. The saw broke through on one side of the pipe. "There," Ernesto said.

"You've almost got it, Papi!" Violetta said.

Ernesto renewed his efforts. In minutes, he sawed through the rest of the pipe and the end cap fell away. "Bring the lamp." Through the window of the kitchen, the last light of the day was fading.

Violetta turned up the wick on the kerosene lamp and scratched a wooden match on the side of the charcoal stove. She lifted the glass shade, ignited the wick and placed the lamp in the middle of the table. She turned the wick up further and the kitchen was bathed in yellow light.

Ernesto turned the open end of the pipe toward the lamp and peered inside. "What is it, Papi?" Maria asked.

"It looks like a rolled-up paper." He turned the open end of the pipe down toward the table and shook it, but nothing fell out. He inserted his little finger into the pipe and twisted. The paper tightened around his finger, and he dragged it out—it was dry. The caps sealing the ends of the pipe had done their job well. Ernesto unrolled the paper and spread it on the table.

"What is it?"

Ernesto frowned as he tried to make sense of the features on the paper and Tomo frowned, too. "It looks like some sort of drawing." Then he straightened in his chair. "No—it's not a drawing. It's a map!"

Ernesto turned the paper so Violetta could see it. "Look—here's the river and here's the sea! He pointed with a tobacco-stained index finger. "And here! Here are the three large rocks near the river's mouth. And see—here near the rocks, it's marked with an 'X'!"

"*Dios mio*, Papi," Violetta said. "Do you think it could be a treasure map?"

"It *must* be a treasure map!" Ernesto said. "What else could it be?"

Outside the circle of light provided by the lamp there was only soundless darkness. Five faces stared at the brown paper lying on the table and tried to absorb the impact of Roberto's discovery.

"What should we do, Papi?" Violetta said.

Ernesto looked hard at each of them. "I'm not sure, but for now we must not tell a soul about this. We must keep this a secret. Does everyone understand? Don't say anything about this to anyone."

They looked across the table at one another and nodded. They would not breathe a word.

5

Roberto awoke as the sun began to shine through the open window of his bedroom. He lay in his bed being careful that no part of his body touched the mosquito netting draped around it. The open windows allowed cool sea breezes to circulate throughout the house, but they also allowed mosquitoes to circulate freely. Roberto hated them. If any part of his body touched the netting, the mosquitoes would find it and sink their bloodthirsty beaks into him.

He was thinking about the map they'd found inside the pipe and what his father had said about it. He'd seen treasure in the motion pictures his mother had taken him to see…especially, the ones about pirates with gold and jewels spilling out of old chests.

Violetta lay on her side and watched her husband think. Ernesto lay on his back, staring up through the mosquito netting at the ceiling. She watched the hair on his chest rise and fall with his breathing.

"Today, we'll have a picnic," Ernesto said.

"A picnic?"

"*Sí*. It's Sunday. We'll make no one curious."

"Down by the Taoro?"

"Yes. We'll fish and cast the net for shrimp. And, for fun, we'll dig holes and bury each other in the sand."

"Where the 'X' is? By the rocks?"

"*Sí*. Where the 'X' is."

Violetta smiled and stroked her hand down her husband's chest. She knew he would think of something.

Roberto would wait a while before he left the safety of the mosquito netting. Many were still clinging to the outside of it. He could hear others still buzzing in a high-pitched whine around his bedroom. Soon, the sun would chase them away and he'd pump the water tank on the roof full and then run down to the beach to see what the night had left behind. Maria would come and join him and probably Tomo and they'd walk together down the beach looking for things of interest. They wouldn't stay long on the beach today, though, because they would want to get back to the house and see what Papi was going to do about the treasure map.

When the children and Tomo returned to the house, Ernesto was sitting at the table eating *chorizo* sausage and eggs. Violetta was still sleeping, so he'd cooked his own breakfast. They craned their heads through the open window, and he grinned up at them with his full chewing mouth. "*Buenos dias*, Papi!"

"*Buenos dias,*" he said. No one could stop smiling…it was going to be an exciting day.

"What are we going to do, Papi?" Maria said.

Ernesto dabbed at the last of his breakfast with a piece of bread. "We're going to have a picnic," he said.

"A picnic!" they shouted. "A picnic, a picnic!"

"Shush, you'll wake your mother," Ernesto said.

It was too late. Violetta shuffled into the kitchen. She wiped the night from her eyes and smiled at their grinning faces. "Do you want *espresso*, Papi?" she said.

"*Sí, por favor. Gracias.*"

Violetta began to heat water on the charcoal stove for the *espresso*. "Mami!" the children shouted. "We're going on a picnic!"

"We are?" she said. "Nobody asked me."

"But Mami! Can we go, Mami? Can we? Please?"

"Does everyone have their jobs finished?"

"*Sí*, Mami, *sí*!"

"Okay," she said. "Then we can have a picnic."

"Tomo," Ernesto said. "Bring the shovel from the coal bin behind the house and lean it near the door."

"But Papi," Tomo said, "the stove is full. I just filled it this morning."

"Bring the shovel," Ernesto said, again.

"*Sí*, Papi," Tomo said.

"Mami, what can we take to eat for our picnic?" Ernesto said.

"There's enough *ropa vieja* left over from last night to make sandwiches for everybody. Maria, pick some oranges. Machito, find us a couple of good coconuts."

6

Sergeant Alfredo Gomez rose from his paperwork and looked out on the day from inside *El Cuartel*, the military headquarters in Santa Fe. It was Sunday—a day when you'd think that everything would be quiet…a day when people went to church and spent time at home with their families. But it was also the day of the week that most people didn't work, so they had free time to spend and that created the potential for trouble. Gomez sighed. Sundays could be difficult if someone began to drink too much. There could be arguments among families, between neighbors, or at the baseball games. Sergeant Gomez hated Sundays.

One of the reasons he hated Sundays was because he was the only one on duty. He was paid for the full week, while the rest of the garrison was not. If there was big trouble, he could call for reinforcements and they'd eventually arrive, but it could take hours.

Sometimes he wondered if he was going to spend the rest of his life in this sleepy little beach town. He'd worked hard to raise himself up from his humble beginnings back in the hills to become sergeant of this military headquarters. But would he ever get the break that would allow him to move to Havana? That's where the real action was. Gomez longed for the opportunities he imagined existing in Havana. Nothing of importance ever happened in Santa Fe.

Another problem with this little town was its lack of attractive, single women. If they were pretty, they were usually already married to a local man. Gomez was both an outsider and a *"federalista."* The townspeople didn't trust him and that disturbed him. "It's true that the government of Presidente Batista is corrupt, but that isn't my fault, is it? That's the way governments are. Why should people expect anything different? Yes, the citizenry thinks I'm cruel, but that's my job. You can't keep control in a town like this if you don't have a heavy hand. There are no *policia* and I'm the only law. Besides, women want a strong man and men respect such a man." Gomez drew in a deep breath and stretched his arms. Yes, I am respected by men and desired by women and as soon as I finish this paperwork, I'll put on my hat and go out on patrol. His ultimate destination would be the beach. Maybe there would be a pretty woman there.

If there were no women at the beach, he could always go see the fat girl later. When the fat girl's mother had first been arrested, Gomez had considered exchanging the woman's release for sexual favors. She wasn't very good-looking, but she could have satisfied him for a while. Then the woman's teenage daughter came to visit her mother at the jail. The daughter's facial features were no more attractive than her mother's and she was too plump, but there was something in the girl's blossoming youthfulness that stirred Gomez.

The mother had been amenable to his visits at their home in exchange for her release from jail and now his visits there had become a weekly regularity. At first, the girl was timid and embarrassed by Gomez's advances, but over time she'd become enthusiastic and was now even petulant when he failed to show for more than a week. Yes, if nothing interesting turned up at the beach today, he'd go see the fat girl tonight.

7

"All right, let's go," Ernesto said when everything was ready. They filed out of the house behind him and trudged down to the beach and along the shoreline to the river. In addition to the picnic lunch, they had two fishing poles, a machete and a shrimp net. Tomo carried the coal shovel on his shoulder.

When they reached the big rocks, Violetta arranged the blankets, so they'd be able to catch the ocean breeze. Ernesto cut some broad-leafed palmetto branches with the machete and pushed their stems down into the sand to provide shade from the hot sun.

Maria and Tomo took the shrimp net and walked along the riverbank. Ernesto and Roberto went around to the other side of the rocks by the river with the fishing poles. They turned over stones along the edge of the stream bed and gathered grubs and worms to put on their hooks for bait. Then they dug two holes in the sand and stacked a pile of rocks around each. Ernesto cast the lines out as far as he could into the river. Then they stuck the ends of the poles into the holes they'd made and pressed the stones tight around them to hold them fast. Ernesto stood back to eye their work. "Okay, Machito?"

"Looks good to me," Roberto said.

Ernesto stole a quick glance around them. He wanted to avoid looking suspicious. So far, it appeared they were succeeding. There were few people at the beach this day and no one seemed to have taken any notice of them. It was time to get to work.

"Keep an eye on our lines, Machito," Ernesto said. "Shout, if we hook a big one." Roberto climbed up on one of the rocks, where he could keep one eye on the fishing lines and one on his father.

Ernesto took one more look around. Then he picked up the coal shovel and began to dig. He started two meters out from the rocks and worked his way along the edge of them. The sand was deep here near the rocks, perhaps five meters higher than the surface of the river. The digging was easy. Soon the hole was waist-high, and he began to work his way out from the rocks. There was no breeze down in the hole and no shade. The tropical sun rose over him. He became drenched with sweat and began to tire, but he didn't stop. He wanted to hear the sound of the shovel striking something hard. It could happen at any moment. He'd been fooled a couple of times by rocks in the sand, but so far, no treasure chest.

"Papi, you must rest," Violetta said. "Stop for a while and we'll have some lunch."

She was right. It was time for a break. The cool sea air struck him the moment he crawled out of the hole. He panted in the shade of a palmetto frond and enjoyed the feel of the fresh air on his skin and in his lungs.

"I think I'll wash myself off and then we can eat," he said to Violetta.

"Okay, Papi. Bring Maria and Tomo when you come back."

Roberto called from his perch on top of the rock. "Can I come, Papi?"

"*Sí*," Ernesto said. "Let's all have a swim. The fish will wait for us." He pulled a laughing Violetta to her feet and the three of them jogged down to the water. The waves were small, and they stayed near the shore where Roberto could touch the bottom. Maria and Tomo dropped their shrimp net and joined the splashing. They had this stretch of beach to themselves.

"Is anybody hungry?" Violetta said.

"Last one to the blankets has to finish digging the hole!" Ernesto said. He turned and began to run back through the water to the beach. Soon Maria and Roberto were out in front with Violetta close behind, everyone squealing as they raced for the blankets. Ernesto slowed to a trot and began walking back up to the blankets with the slow-moving Tomo. When they neared the blankets, Tomo broke into a waddling run to get there first and laughed with the trick he'd pulled on Ernesto.

Violetta was passing out the sandwiches when Roberto yelled from the top of the rocks. "Come quickly, Papi! We're catching something!" Ernesto ran to the river, followed by everyone but Tomo, who remained on the blankets eating his *ropa vieja* sandwich.

One of the rods was bent double and had almost been pulled out from its hole. "It's a big one, Machito! This is the biggest fish I've ever seen!" Ernesto walked down the bank with the rod to ease the pressure on the line. They crowded around him, anxious to catch a glimpse of the big fish.

8

It was nearly noon before Sergeant Gomez finished his paperwork. The garrison was getting hot, and he was ready for some fresh air. He knew he looked good when he stepped into the street. His uniform was clean. His tall leather boots were polished to a shiny black. His hat was on straight and serious. Anyone who saw him would know that he meant business and anyone who spoke to him would do so with respect.

With the sun straight up there wasn't much shade, as he walked down the main street of Santa Fe. He stopped at *La Bodeguita,* but it was still quiet. There were only a couple of patrons who stared back at him with disinterest. He'd stop back later when the heat of the day had cooled. People who'd been drinking at home would become expansive. They'd need an audience for their drunken opinions and begin to drift into the bar. By evening, it would be full.

With the town quiet, Sergeant Gomez decided it was time to check the beach. He was still a block away when he began to feel the cool breeze blowing in from the water. He found his favorite bench in the shade of a palm tree and looked out at the rippling blue expanse. There weren't many people there, today. Perhaps the heat had people feeling lazy. He looked up and down the beach. All couples and families—no single women. That was disappointing, but it was still nice to sit in the shade and feel the breeze on his face. He was about to remove his hat when something strange near the river caught his eye.

It was only a man, sitting on a blanket eating a sandwich, but next to him was a large pile of sand. Odd. That pile hadn't been there before. Sergeant Gomez studied this curiosity for a moment and decided to investigate.

Tomo was absorbed in his sandwich when a long shadow fell across the blanket. He took another bite as his eyes followed the shadow back to the tall black boots riveted in the sand at the edge of the blanket. He stopped chewing and his eyes moved upward to the impressive military uniform of Sergeant Gomez. Tomo couldn't see the sergeant's face, which Gomez had placed in line with the sun, but he'd seen these boots and the uniform before. They frightened him. He'd heard the stories of cruelty that circulated among the villagers about the garrison, so when he saw the boots, the uniform and the long shadow standing over him, he was afraid.

Sergeant Gomez gestured to the hole and the pile of sand. "What is this?"

Tomo wanted to answer, but his mouth was full of sandwich, and he didn't know what to say. He chewed hard and fast, but his mouth had become dry, and he was having trouble swallowing. He looked around for water.

Gomez was used to having people straighten with attention when he addressed them, especially when he was wearing his Sunday uniform, but this man wasn't responding. "What is this!" he said again.

Tomo found a corked bottle of water among the things Violetta had packed. He raised it to his lips and took a quick drink to help him swallow the remains of the sandwich. He raised it once more to help with the last swallow, but a blow from the uniformed figure knocked the bottle from his hand. The soldier stepped onto the blanket and screamed in his face.

"Why is this hole here? I won't ask you again!" What was wrong with this fat pig of a man? Was he crazy? Couldn't he see who he was? Couldn't he see he was about to be in trouble with his authority?

Tomo began to tremble and cry. The fat of his shirtless body quivered with the fear he was feeling. Where were Ernesto and Violetta? "Treasure!" It was all he could think of to say.

"Treasure? What treasure?" Gomez said. His tone turned from irate to curious. Sergeant Gomez also gleaned from the child-like appearance of the man under stress and the meek tenor of his voice when he cried out his single word that he was probably not trying to be difficult. This man was just stupid.

"Map!" Tomo blurted.

"Map? What map?"

"In the pipe."

"Pipe?" Sergeant Gomez squatted down next to Tomo and began to speak to him in a gentle tone. He picked up the bottle of water he'd slapped from Tomo's hand. It was still half full, and he handed it back to him. "Tell me about this pipe,"

Tomo had nearly finished relating the story to Sergeant Gomez when the rest of the family returned. He told how he and the children had found the pipe with the strange cross on its side and how Ernesto had sawn off the end of the pipe and reached in with his little finger and drawn out a map. And he told how it had been decided that they would have a picnic today and dig for the treasure.

Ernesto had nearly landed the big fish. But just as he brought it near to the shore, the fish glimpsed the source of its misery and with a final desperate effort gave a shake of his broad head and broke free. Now, as Ernesto walked with Violetta and the children back to the blanket, they were all talking about the big fish and how close they'd come to catching it.

Ernesto stopped walking when he saw Sergeant Gomez squatting in front of Tomo. The uniformed sergeant was listening and nodding, as Tomo told his tale. Ernesto's heart sank. The game was over. The entire affair had seemed an improbable endeavor from the beginning and had become even more doubtful with each unrewarded shovelful of sand, but it was a dream that had to be pursued in the hope that it might come true. Now, it would all be taken from them.

Sergeant Gomez rose from his conversation with Tomo when Ernesto approached the blanket. Violetta and the children huddled behind him. The two men looked hard at one another.

"This man has told me of the map," Gomez said. "Let me see it."

Ernesto despised this officious bastard. The *militarios* from *El Cuartel* were just goons employed by the government to keep the people in line. They weren't there to protect the people, but to enforce the will of Batista's dictatorship. There was nothing he could do but obey. He'd be lucky to not be arrested. He pulled the pipe and the map from the bag where he'd hidden them and handed them to the sergeant.

Gomez examined both the pipe and the map. He traced the outline of the cross on the side of the pipe with his index finger. He studied the map for a few moments and then looked at the terrain around them. He, too, noted the similarity between the three large rocks on the map near the river and the place where they now stood. He reconnected with Ernesto's glare. "You know," he said, "there are serious penalties for not reporting such things to the government. If there is a treasure here, it belongs to the people of Cuba, not to the man who finds it."

If he hadn't been so angry, Ernesto would have laughed. The chances of the people of Cuba ever receiving any benefit from a possible treasure were now even more remote than the chances of finding the treasure in the first place. If a treasure was ever unearthed, it would be confiscated by the government, alright, but it would never be seen again. "*Sí*," he said, "if we'd found anything, we would have reported it, immediately."

Sergeant Gomez considered his best course of action. If he arrested these men, he'd have to make a report and then there'd be a written record of the incident. If he let them all go, there would be no record. "You've found nothing?" he said. He knew the answer to this question but asked it anyway. If anything had been found, they wouldn't have left it to go fishing.

"No, we haven't found anything," Ernesto said.

"Who else knows about this?"

"No one." Ernesto could read what the sergeant was thinking. He didn't like the thought of Gomez finding the treasure, but this could be his way out of the situation, too. If Gomez wanted to keep this a secret with an eye toward personal gain, then Ernesto wouldn't be arrested.

"Fill in your hole and go home," Gomez said. "I'll have this area excavated, tomorrow. If anything of value is found, you have my personal guarantee that you'll be rewarded for having led us to it."

"*Sí*," Ernesto said. "*Muchas gracias, sargento*." Ernesto was certain that he would never see so much as a single peso of reward, but there was nothing he could do.

Although few people had come to the beach on this day, some had taken notice of the controversy and a small crowd had gathered. "Clear this area at once," Gomez said. "Immediately! There's nothing for you to see here. This is a matter for the Cuban government."

9

Gomez sat back at his bench in the shade of the palm tree and watched Ernesto fill in the hole. He hadn't risen from his humble beginnings to the rank of sergeant by accident. It was his habit to study all situations which presented themselves with an eye toward determining what possible advantage might be extracted from them. And then he studied some more, to see how things might best be arranged to obtain maximum benefit for himself. This part of his planning began with deciding what benefit it was that he wanted most. In this case there was a possible fortune, yes, but fortune could always be turned into opportunity.

What he desired, even more than money, was power. He wanted to be assigned a position of authority in Havana. It was his lifelong dream. It was true that money could exert influence and sometimes buy power for a man, but money could be taken from you. On the other hand, if a man had power, then he was in a position to get money. Power could be taken from you, too, but a truly smart and ambitious man could always find a way to stay near the seat of power until such time that he could once again have it fully within his grasp.

There was also the problem of the excavation. The quickest way would be with a steam shovel. There was only one man in town with such an expensive machine and Gomez had nothing on him. There was no threat he could hold over the man's head to ensure his silence. The owner of the steam shovel had some power of his own and would need to be dealt with. Gomez could offer to split whatever was found with him, but what if the man couldn't be trusted? Even if the man agreed to the collusion and didn't report him, there was a chance that someone would find out and Gomez's career would be ruined. He didn't like taking chances. He preferred calculated near-certainties and to this end he had learned to trust no one.

No, if he found a treasure, it would be better to arrange a deal with the highest-ranking authority he knew. There was no official of the government who wouldn't jump at the chance for riches, especially if the only cost to the official would be to promote an obscure sergeant from a small town. But whom could he approach? The highest-ranking official he knew personally was Colonel Hernando Villanueva. Colonel Villanueva was the chief of security for *El Presidente* Batista and a very powerful man. Gomez knew him because he'd once saved the colonel's daughter from drowning at the beach.

It was customary for men of wealth and position to allow their families to escape from the heat of Havana in summer. Santa Fe was popular for summer bungalows and an easy visit for the men on weekends and holidays. Colonel Villanueva's wife had been at the beach with their three-year-old daughter, watching the girl as she played in the shallows. Suddenly, the water drained away from the beach, leaving a wide expanse of sea bottom exposed. Moments later, a rogue wave, several times the size of a normal wave, crashed onto the shore, engulfed the girl, and swept her out to sea.

Gomez had only been a corporal then. He was patrolling the beach when he heard the distress cries of *señora* Villanueva. He stripped down and dove in after the child. He rescued the girl and returned her to her mother's arms. The act hadn't been difficult, but the girl's mother had lavished praise upon him, called him a "hero" and reported his "bravery" to her husband.

Colonel Villanueva made a special trip out from Havana to Santa Fe to pin a medal on him and even promoted him to sergeant. Gomez smiled as he remembered the moment. The colonel had impressed him with his imperious bearing and competent manner. Yes, if he uncovered a treasure, he'd try approaching Colonel Villanueva.

Gomez turned his attention to the map. Both the pipe with its Spanish cross on the side and the map appeared to be genuine. But the family had said they found the pipe near the mouth of the river. Why would someone bury a treasure and then leave the clue to its location less than a hundred meters from the supposed burial spot? This didn't make sense.

Sergeant Gomez put his hands behind his head and leaned back on the bench with his feet outstretched and his boots crossed. No matter. He smiled and breathed deeply of the cool ocean air. Who cared how it had gotten there? The important thing was for him to find it, if it was there, and use it to advance his position. Yes, if he did manage to find a treasure, he'd contact Colonel Villanueva. Villanueva was an important connection and could help him to parlay a treasure into something more. Perhaps his luck had finally turned. It was about time.

10

Alyssa Villanueva raced her cousin to the door to answer the heavy knocking. It had been more than a week since she, her mother and her cousin, José, had left Havana and come to Santa Fe for the summer and she was hoping for it to be her father. When she swung the door open, she was both surprised and disappointed to see a tall, uniformed stranger. She was used to seeing men in uniform back in Havana coming and going from their house, but it seemed somehow out of place here at their vacation cottage.

"I'm *sargento* Gomez," the soldier said. "I'd like to speak to your mother, *por favor*."

"*Sí, señor*," Alyssa said. "Mami," she called. "A man is here to see you."

"Who is it my child?"

"He's a sergeant."

Juliana Villanueva enjoyed coming to their little cottage in Santa Fe. They not only left the stifling summer heat of Havana, but she also escaped the demanding social obligations that came with being a colonel's wife. Coming to Santa Fe was like stepping back into a simpler time. A visit from a soldier here at the cottage was irritating. She put down her reading and went to the door with an unhappy demeanor, until she recognized her visitor. "*Sargento* Gomez!" she said. "Don't you know who this is, Alyssa? This is the man who saved your life. This is our brave hero, Sergeant Gomez. Come in, *Sargento*, come in."

Gomez stepped inside. "*Gracias, señora*," he said. He beamed with the adoration he was receiving from this woman of means.

Juliana ushered him into the living area. "It's so good to see you, *Sargento*. Let me get you some coffee. Have you been well?"

"*Sí, señora, gracias*," Gomez said. "Thank you for the coffee, but I can't stay long."

They sat at a small table in the living area to have their coffee. Juliana had been so happy to see the savior of her only child that she only now began to wonder about the purpose of his visit. "We haven't seen you for two years," she said.

"*Sí, señora*," Gomez said. He looked across the table and studied her pretty features. Colonel Villanueva was a lucky man; she was a lovely woman. He searched for small talk. "I've always wondered, *señora*, how it is that you have blonde hair?"

Juliana's hand went to her hair and smoothed it with a pleased, self-conscious smile. She was proud of her hair and her heritage. "I'm Jewish, *Sargento*. I escaped here to Cuba with my parents and my sister from Poland just before the Nazis invaded."

Gomez nodded, "Ah." He measured his words, not wanting to seem too anxious or presumptuous with the wife of the important man from whom he planned to ask a favor. "And the little girl, she has been well?" he asked, reminding Juliana of his importance in their lives, while maintaining an air of professional concern for the family.

"*Sí*," Juliana said. "She's growing up quickly. She still loves to play in the water and is still a risk-taker, but she understands the power and capriciousness of the sea and is more cautious around it now. And how have *you* been Sergeant? You're looking well."

Gomez smiled with her recognition of the care he took in his dress and presentment. "*Gracias, señora. Sí*, I'm doing very well, but I wonder if I might impose upon your extreme kindness to ask a small favor of you?"

"Of course, how may I help you, Sergeant Gomez?"

"I have a private matter that I'd like to discuss with Colonel Villanueva. Due to its sensitive nature, I'd prefer to not go through military channels."

"May I ask what it is that you'd like to talk with my husband about?" Her husband adored her. He would accede to nearly any request she made of him and would ultimately tell her everything that transpired during this meeting being proposed by Sergeant Gomez. But she was curious herself about what this "matter" could be. "He'll want to know its importance."

"I'm sorry, *señora*," Gomez said, "but I think it best if I do not say. With all sincere respect to you and your kindness, I believe it's better for all concerned if I share my situation only with him."

"*Sí*," she said. "I understand." If the sergeant wasn't comfortable sharing his secret with her, there was no sense pressing him any further. Hernando would tell her all about it afterward, anyway. "My husband is scheduled to come out to the cottage this weekend. I'll tell him then of your request, Sergeant Gomez."

Gomez smiled broadly. "*Muchas gracias, señora!*" He'd been nervous about coming to see *señora* Villanueva and asking this favor of her. The stakes were high. But now he'd done it and it had gone well.   The composure he'd maintained throughout their conversation had slipped only a little with his excitement and relief when she had said 'yes,' but he caught himself now and regained a dignified posture. "I'll remain at El Cuartel all weekend awaiting a signal from him. I think it best if we meet somewhere other than my humble headquarters. There isn't enough privacy there."

"I'll tell him," Juliana said. She was filled with curiosity about what could possibly be this man's need to speak with her husband in such secrecy. But she accepted that she'd just have to wait until the weekend.

"*Muchas gracias*," Gomez said again. "Thank you for your interest and for the coffee. You've been very kind, *señora* Villanueva." He rose and moved toward the door.

"You're most welcome, Sergeant Gomez. *Vaya con Dios*, go with God." Juliana closed the door behind him and smiled. This secret intrigued her, and Hernando would soon be sharing it with her. She was certain he'd be unable to resist her entreaties.

Outside the Villanueva's cottage, Alfredo Gomez was smiling, too. The visit had gone well. His plan was in motion.

11

Colonel Hernando Villanueva stood looking out the window of his second-floor office, down onto the *Malecón*, the boulevard that ran along the waterfront of Havana. From this vantage point, the gently curving roadway looked like the stroke of an artist's brush painted against the blue background of the sea.

His official position was Chief of Security, but Colonel Villanueva had many responsibilities within the government. His primary role was to select and train men to guard Batista. Keeping *El Presidente* safe was not easy. The man had accumulated many enemies over the years. Villanueva also supervised the gathering of intelligence information throughout Cuba. There were many eager informers and very little escaped the colonel's notice. In addition, Batista often called upon Villanueva to deal with special problems like the young man who was currently sitting in his office. A student at the University of Havana, the man had been brought before Villanueva for stirring up the student body and fomenting talk of revolution against Batista and his government.

The student was an inexhaustible talker and continued to rant about corruption in the Batista regime and inequities in Cuban society, even after Villanueva had turned his back upon him to revisit a cigar in an ashtray on the windowsill. The colonel had smoked nearly two-thirds of it earlier and was down to the final remains. This was his favorite part of the cigar because it always tasted the sweetest. He struck a match and re-lit it. The breeze through the open window caught the smoke and swirled it away when he exhaled.

The student was not incorrect in his impassioned statements. There *was* great disparity between the wealthy and the poor in Cuba. There was also much corruption in the government that seemed to worsen daily. The arrogance of Bastista and his inner circle had grown along with the solidification of *El Presidente's* power. It disturbed Villanueva that the privileged had begun to view themselves as untouchable. Their excesses were becoming increasingly blatant. American businesses enabled a thriving economy in Cuba, but they commanded too much influence and not everyone benefited. There was also the problem of the American mafia that had entered the country along with the gambling casinos. Due to the self-absorbed attitudes of Batista and those in the upper classes, the plight of lower-class Cubans tended to be ignored.

Villanueva, however, strove to remain a principled and moral man, doing what he could in his position to alleviate wrongs and assist his countrymen. He was passionate about Cuba and was as sickened by the moral deterioration around him as the young idealist sitting in his office. He put his cigar back in the ashtray on the windowsill and turned to face the student who was still talking. Villanueva held up a hand to silence him, but without effect.

"*Señor*!" Villanueva shouted. "*Silencio*!" The young man's voice trailed off. "Look, Fidel," Villanueva said when the student had quieted. "I know that you come from a good family. I personally believe that some of the ideas you propose may even have some merit, but I also know that you will not effect the changes you want through rebellion. You cannot be successful in such a fight. You'll only end up dead or in prison. You're obviously an intelligent young man. A bit verbose, but I believe your heart is in the right place and you have much to offer Cuba. Have you ever considered the field of law? You're a fine speaker. With such a degree you could embrace many of these causes and help the disadvantaged by working within the system instead of against it."

The young man said nothing but tilted his head slightly and Villanueva could tell he was considering his suggestion. The student stood, his cap held in his hands, and looked down at Villanueva. Villanueva was a tall man, but the student was at least two inches taller. Villanueva gave him a pat on the back as he walked him from his office. "Give my idea some serious thought," he said. "I'd hate to see a bright young man like yourself come to a bad end." Neither of them said anything more and the student left the office. He seemed to be weighing Villanueva's recommendation.

Villanueva returned to his desk but was followed back into his office by his lieutenant adjutant. "There's another man here to see you…a *carbonero*." The lieutenant's voice registered disgust.

Villanueva sighed.   He was as much fatigued by his adjutant's elitist attitude, as he was by the endless line of people with problems who filed through his office. "Show him in," he said.

"*Sientesé, por favor*," Villanueva said when the *carbonero* entered, motioning the man toward one of the office's leather chairs, despite the sooty appearance of his clothing. The colonel extended his hand in greeting, while noting the hands of his visitor. Years of delivering coal had left them stained, despite a recent attempt to clean them prior to the carbonero's audience with the colonel.

"*Gracias, señor*," the man said, taking the seat.

"How can I help you?" Villanueva asked.

"*Señor*," the man began, "I have come because I've been told that you are a friend to many people. I am a poor *carbonero*. I have a wife and two small children. I work from before it becomes light in the morning until after dark, delivering the charcoal. My wife washes clothes brought to her by wealthy women. We are barely able to keep food on the table for ourselves and our children. Now, they tell me that I will have to pay a tax on my horse and my cart. They tell me of a law that any deliveryman who owns a horse and cart must pay a tax to use the roads. I cannot afford this tax. What can I do?"

Villanueva smiled. The one good thing about a corrupt bureaucracy was that, while it was much too easy to interpret the laws in favor of taking unfair advantage of people, it was just as easy to bend them to help someone like the *carbonero*. "*Sí*," Villanueva said. "I can help you. Give the horse and the cart to your wife. Since your wife will not be using the horse and cart to deliver anything, she will not have to pay the tax. If you deliver your coal, but do not own the horse and cart, you will not have to pay the tax. This is the law. Do as I say, and you'll have no more trouble."

As the man digested the colonel's words, his look of desperation faded, and wonderment emerged. Villanueva's suggestion was so simple and so easy. The *carbonero* rose from his chair, smiling and nodding. "*Gracias, señor*," he said, as he backed out of Villanueva's office. "*Muchas gracias!*"

Juliana cooked *boliche* for Hernando's arrival Friday evening. A roast stuffed with sausage, peppers, garlic, onions and tomato sauce and served with black beans and rice. It was his favorite meal. He'd now be putty in her hands. She waited until he had had two glasses of rioja before she mentioned the sergeant's visit.

"Do you remember Sergeant Gomez?" Juliana said, taking a sip of her own wine while watching the eyes of her husband.

"The corporal who pulled Alyssa out of the water, whom I promoted to Sergeant? *Sí*, of course," Colonel Villanueva said, concentrating on his meal. No *boliche* could match Juliana's and he was sick of military and restaurant food.

"I talked to him this week," Juliana said.

Hernando stopped eating for a moment. He drained the remainder of the *rioja* in his glass and looked across the table at his wife. "Tell me, *mí cielo* how is the sergeant?"

"He came to ask about Alyssa and said that he wants to talk to you."

"He came here? To our private cottage?" Colonel Villanueva was incredulous. "He wants to talk to me? He knows he must go through proper military channels. He shouldn't be addressing his problems with me. An enlisted man coming to my home and intruding upon my wife is disgraceful. Any concerns he has should be submitted to his immediate superior. A man in my position is involved with far greater issues than any troubles a small-town sergeant might have. I will give no notice to his request."

Juliana poured more wine into her husband's glass. Hernando was a proper military man and she had expected his reaction to be thus. This was why she'd prepared the *boliche* and opened the *rioja*. They were designed to soften his tough military exterior and allow her to reach his tender qualities, which she knew to lay just beneath the surface. "Let us not forget that he saved the life of our daughter," she said. "And it's my impression that Sergeant Gomez's concern is not purely a military one. He said that he must talk only with you and in private. He said that no one else can know of your communication together, which is why he didn't go through the proper military channels."

Hernando raised his glass to his lips and stared across the table at his wife. She smiled back at him in a way that told him he would soon have no choice but to agree, not to Gomez's request, but to hers. "What is this difficulty he has?"

"He wouldn't tell me," Juliana said. "He told me he could share it only with you."

Villanueva sighed in resignation. This would be against all military protocol, but Gomez *had* saved his daughter from drowning. Perhaps he did owe the man something. If it was what Juliana wanted, he could give the man a few moments. "Alright, he said, "I'll go by the garrison tomorrow."

"He said that he couldn't talk to you there," Juliana said. "He stressed that your conversation must be in complete privacy."

"What can this man want?" Villanueva said, stabbing at his food. "This is just too much, Juliana." He looked up to see her still smiling across the table at him. "You will give me no peace, will you? Okay, tell the sergeant to meet me here at the cottage, tomorrow."

12

Sergeant Gomez sat alone inside El Cuartel waiting for word from Villanueva. He was nervous. He'd been nervous ever since the man with the steam shovel had unearthed the treasure chest. Gomez had cordoned off the area and arranged for the man to do some digging at the beach. He'd designed a ruse to keep the man from becoming suspicious. He told him they'd be performing a preliminary investigation for the government. The government needed to know how deep a trench needed to be dug in order to reach bedrock. They were considering the establishment of a port in Santa Fe, but they must first know the geology of the area near the river. As a first step, the government had ordered Sergeant Gomez to do some digging in the area. He warned the man with the steam shovel that he shouldn't expect to be paid right away. He told him that if everything went satisfactorily, however, the government was likely to give him some large contracts in the future. There was the possibility that this project would prove very lucrative to the man down the road.

Gomez smiled. Greed, it makes men lose their senses. Even intelligent men can be led to ignore the obvious, if they are blinded by the prospect of easy money. The man had come the next day with his steam shovel to begin digging near the big rocks. Gomez roped off the area to keep prying eyes away. He sat on one of the big rocks while the man worked, enduring the deafening roars and clanking that the steam shovel produced. Its metal teeth dug into the beach, lifting load after load of dripping wet sand and mud and swung it around on cables before dropping it onto a growing pile. The great metal beast gradually ate away sand deposited by centuries of ocean waves.

Gomez hoped to see a big, rusty, sea chest come toppling out of the steam shovel's bucket on one of its turns. But each bucketful produced only more sand, mud, bits of coral and seashells.

The steam shovel operator stopped for lunch and returned later that afternoon, only to achieve the same results. Now, over half of the beach near the rocks had been excavated to a depth of five meters. Could the treasure be even deeper? Gomez began to wonder at what point he should give up and end the search. Would he have the man dig halfway to China? Should he tell him to begin excavating further out from the rocks? The "X" marked on the map was near the rocks. Could it be that the dimensions were not accurate? Gomez began to walk around the muddy mountain. He picked up a long stick and poked holes in the side of the mound.

And then he saw it. It wasn't the big sea chest he'd imagined, but a small one. It was perched right side up, sitting almost jauntily atop a chunk of sea coral. Although it was covered in mud, Gomez was able to recognize the shape as a man-made one, perhaps twice the size of a man's lunch box. Specks of tarnished blue-green bronze peeked through the muck.

Gomez scrambled up the slope. His boots sank to their tops in the loose debris of the pile. He hopped and slid his way back down with the box tucked under one arm. His eyes darted around for witnesses. There were none. He'd done it! He had the treasure and no one else knew about it! The steam shovel operator continued noisily on, absorbed in his task and oblivious to Gomez's good fortune.

Gomez wrapped the box in a blanket he'd brought along to cloak a large chest, carried it back to El Cuartel and locked it in the safe. Then he'd gone to visit *señora* Villanueva to arrange a meeting with her husband.

Gomez sat the little chest on the desk in front of him. While he waited for word from the colonel, he cleaned it off. It had withstood the centuries of burial fairly well. The brass that provided support and protection for its edges and corners had turned milky green, as had the hatch and padlock. He'd discussed with himself the issue of opening the chest since bringing it back to El Cuartel. The box was heavy. He'd shaken it and whatever was inside seemed to move a little, but he was unable to make a reasonable guess about its contents. He was nearly mad with curiosity about what was in it. He didn't think it would be difficult to break the padlock. His primary interest, however, was to use the contents of the chest as a bargaining tool to improve his position in the military. If he opened it, there could be suspicions raised about the authenticity of what it contained. If there were treasure inside, he might even be accused of having stolen some of it for himself.

No, he would not open it now. He would insist, however, on being present when it was opened, lest others make the claim that it held nothing of value.

There was a knock on the door. "*Señor* Sergeant," a small voice called. Gomez opened the door. It was a boy.

"Colonel Villanueva said for you to come to his house at noon, today."

"Anything else?" Gomez said.

"*Sí, señor*. He gave me a peso." The boy grinned and exhibited his prize.

"And who are you?" Gomez said.

"My name is José. *El Colonel* is my uncle."

"*Gracias, muchacho*," Gomez said. He nodded and closed the door. Colonel Villanueva had done well to send a small boy. The secret would remain theirs.

At noon, Sergeant Alfredo Gomez presented himself upon the doorstep of Colonel Hernando Villanueva's summer cottage. He carried a canvas satchel, which he strove to bear as normally as possible to disguise the heavy weight of its contents. "*Buenos tardes*, Sergeant Gomez," Colonel Villanueva said upon opening the door. "Enter." His tone was stiff and official.

"*Buenos tardes*, Colonel," Gomez said. He bowed slightly and stepped inside the cottage.

Colonel Villanueva led him to the same table where the sergeant had had coffee earlier in the week with his wife. The maid had been dismissed for the afternoon to assist in the secrecy Gomez had requested. Colonel Villanueva had sent Juliana and the children to the beach. They would be alone. "There is some coffee," the colonel said. "Would you care for some?" He didn't want to appear too hospitable. This was a rash and presumptuous meeting that Gomez had requested. His offer of the coffee was only good manners.

"*Sí*," Gomez said. He was somewhat surprised by Colonel Villanueva's largess. He, too, was aware that he was treading upon delicate ground in this affair. He was intruding into the colonel's private life. In order to arrange this private meeting, he'd taken advantage of having saved the life of the colonel's daughter. The colonel's formal congeniality was further evidence of this powerful man's self-assured dignity. "*Muchas gracias*, Colonel."

Villanueva placed the coffee in front of Gomez and took a seat across from him. "Now, tell me about this matter," he said.

Gomez had gone over his presentation to Colonel Villanueva many times in his mind. He'd practiced by pretending himself to be seated in front of the colonel's stern and demanding eyes, but the pressure of the reality was even more than he'd imagined. Inside, his stomach was reeling. On the outside, he endeavored to maintain a cool demeanor. What he was asking of the colonel required little more than a slight-of-hand gesture from this powerfully connected man. Delicacy and tact were of the utmost importance. The way Gomez was going about it was designed to allow the colonel room to be dishonest with the state. But it was any presumption of the colonel's corruptibility that needed to be avoided at all costs. Gomez wanted to give Colonel Villanueva the opportunity to be dishonest if he so chose but arrange things so the assumption would be that the colonel was acting honorably.

Gomez began to present the facts, one by one. He pulled the lead pipe from the bag and laid it in front of Colonel Villanueva with the cross facing upward. "This pipe was found at the beach by a little boy," he said. Gomez pointed to the end of the pipe, where Ernesto Valiente had sawn it off. "Rather than report the discovery to the authorities, as he should have, the boy's father sawed off the end of the pipe to see what was inside."

Sergeant Gomez wanted to project an official air and present himself as a responsible employee of the government who was trying to do the right things. Maintaining such an attitude was vital if he was going to be successful in his private quest. "Inside the pipe, the boy's father found this." Gomez reached into the bag and withdrew the map, which he placed in front of Colonel Villanueva.

Villanueva picked up the corroded pipe and examined it. He looked at the end where Ernesto had sawn it through and noted that it had been freshly cut. As others had done before him, he traced the mark of the cross with his finger. He laid the pipe to the side and took the map from Gomez. Spreading it out with his hands, he recognized it as appearing authentic to the time of the Spanish treasure fleets.

Gomez pointed to the river drawn on the map. "You see, here is the Taoro River. And these big rocks along the shore? They're still there. And this 'X'? It marks the location where something was buried."

Colonel Villanueva nodded slowly. Where was this all leading? He remained silent, while Gomez continued his story.

"I found the man digging there last Sunday. He hadn't found anything, yet. I told him to stop and commanded any onlookers to leave immediately. I roped off the area and hired a man with a steam shovel to come in and excavate it. To keep anything that was found safe for the government, I didn't tell the owner of the steam shovel that he might be digging for buried treasure."

Villanueva looked up from the map into the eyes of Sergeant Gomez and nodded that he understood his attempt at secrecy to protect the find from the unscrupulous. Gomez was either a fanatical government supporter or a clever opportunist. Villanueva couldn't decide which. "What did you find?" he said. The colonel assumed that Gomez must have found something, or he would not be here.

"I expected that if we found something, it would be a large sea chest," Gomez said. "So, I kept watching for one to appear as the man dug with his steam shovel. But then I saw a little chest."

"Where is this chest?" Villanueva said.

"I have it here," Gomez said. He lifted the padlocked box out of the canvas bag and placed it on the table before Colonel Villanueva.

Villanueva stared at the chest. What a fantastic thing. This mysterious chest appeared to have lain hidden beneath the sand for hundreds of years and now had just landed in the middle of his table. "The lock is still intact. You haven't opened it?" Villanueva said.

"*No, señor.*" Gomez knew that this had to be the most convincing part of his presentation to the Colonel. "Whatever is in this box belongs to the people of Cuba." He wanted to sound matter of fact and not transparently self-righteous. "This is why I didn't take this matter to my immediate superior, whom I do not trust. You, however, Colonel Villanueva, I believe to be the most honorable and trustworthy man in all the government. I was certain you'd know how to do the right thing."

Villanueva again looked up from the chest to study the eyes of Sergeant Gomez. This man had had the contents of this box all to himself and had not opened it. Instead, he had sought him out to "do the right thing" with it for "the people of Cuba." Perhaps Juliana was right, and this man really was a hero. "That's the question, *sargento*," Villanueva said. "What is the right thing? As you seem to be aware, there are many in the government who believe that *they* are 'the people of Cuba' and would try to get all or part of whatever is in this box for themselves."

"*Sí, señor.*"

"I think it's time we find out what's in this chest," Villanueva said. "If I'm to do the right thing with it, it's important to know how valuable its contents really are."

"*Sí,*" Gomez said. "I brought a crowbar and a hammer. I thought you might wish to find out what's inside."

Once more Villanueva had reason to look hard at this man and attempt to discern his true intentions. Sergeant Gomez gave the appearance of a simple and honest man, but his thinking processes were so clever that he gave the colonel pause to wonder. He took the crowbar from Gomez, inserted it inside the hasp of the lock and twisted. The entire lock assembly detached from the soft, salt-water impregnated wood of the box. He then drove the tapered end of the bar into the space between the box and its lid and pried. He did this several times in different places around the box. He returned to the front of the chest and again drove the bar deep into the crack. Gomez came around the table and watched over his shoulder. The colonel pried up the lid once more and this time it separated from the box. The tarnished and encrusted brass hinges, however, were frozen and refused to rotate. Gomez helped Villanueva pry the lid up until the hinges broke free. The lid clattered across the table and onto the floor.

"*Jesus Crist*," Villanueva said, as he gazed upon the contents of the little box.

"*Dios mio*," Gomez said.

"*Fantastico*."

"*Increible*."

Following their initial expulsions, both men remained speechless, as they tried to absorb the sight in front of them. The old chest was brimming with bright, green emeralds.

"This is unbelievable," Villanueva said.

Gomez nodded. He hadn't dreamed that the little chest he'd been protecting for last few days would hold such riches.

They reached their hands into the box, scooped up double handfuls of the jewels and let them trickle through their fingers back into the pile. "They must be worth millions," Villanueva said.

"*Sí*," Gomez said.

"They'll have to be protected from the unscrupulous."

"*Sí*." Gomez didn't really care what the colonel did with the treasure. His sole desire was to become an officer. It wasn't possible in the Cuban military for an enlisted man of no hereditary consequence to reach the rank of officer, unless someone of stature recommended him. This was Gomez's fervent hope.

"We must each swear to secrecy," Villanueva said. "The steam shovel operator knows nothing of this box?"

"No."

"And what of the man who found the pipe?"

I'll tell him that we searched and found nothing," Gomez said.

"Alright, the man probably deserves something, but we can't afford to tell him if we're to maintain this secret. Besides, he tried to get the treasure for himself, didn't he?"

"*Sí*, he did," Gomez said.

"And you, Sergeant," Villanueva said, eyeing Gomez, as he tried to evaluate the reliability of this sly man. "Can you keep this secret?"

"*Sí*," Gomez said. "I can and I will. There is but one favor I'd like to ask of you, *El Colonel*."

Villanueva sat back in his chair. Ah, there *is* something in that clever mind of his and here it comes.

"I want to be an officer."

Villanueva was taken aback. A country bumpkin becoming an officer? Impossible. Preposterous. The colonel had to restrain himself from spitting away the unrealistic request of this presumptuous *campesino*. "You must qualify for the Military Academy," he said. "My word might get you the opportunity, but after that you'd be on your own."

"I can do it," Gomez said.

"The physical tests are demanding for anyone," Villanueva said, "but the intellectual examinations are extremely difficult…even for an educated man."

"It's true that I haven't had the advantages of intensive schooling," Gomez said, "but I've read and taught myself…even the mathematics."

"And if I recommend you, you'll swear to maintain our secrecy?"

"Most assuredly, *El Colonel*."

Villanueva studied the jewels. He didn't want the treasure for himself. He already had money, power, and position. He truly believed the treasure belonged to the people of Cuba. But, if others in the government knew the existence of these jewels, they'd stop at nothing to get their hands on them.

If the colonel did take the unusual step of recommending Sergeant Gomez for academy consideration, there would be some raised eyebrows, but everyone would know that Gomez had saved his daughter's life. That fact, along with Villanueva's powerful position should be sufficient to quash any serious criticism. Besides, the chances of an uneducated peasant from the country passing the entrance examinations were close to zero. Villanueva would only be agreeing to sponsor Gomez's consideration for the academy, not his acceptance into it. That would depend solely upon the man's performance on the physical and academic tests.

"Then I agree to recommend you, Sergeant Gomez," Villanueva said. "You are a hero to my wife and my daughter. You've done the right thing in the handling of this matter of the treasure. I commend you for bringing it to me and wish you good fortune in your endeavor. *Buena suerte, sargento,*" Colonel Villanueva said, rising and offering his hand. "Good luck. You're surely going to need it."

"*Muchas gracias!*" Gomez said. "*Muchas gracias, señor!* I assure you that I will not be a disappointment."

13

Havana, Cuba
September 1957

Alyssa Villanueva sat in her Physics class at the University of Havana. Only half-listening to the *profesore*, she was tracing "José" on the back of her notebook. She felt the stare of a student sitting next to her and allowed her eyes to drift upward into his. He smiled. She gave him a cheerless one in return.

Class dismissed and she began walking home, books clutched to her chest. Without warning, the student appeared next to her.

"I'm Diego Montalvo. You look so sad."

Alyssa kept walking. I never should have smiled at him, she thought. Now, I'll never get rid of him. She stopped and looked up at him. He's so tall. Handsome, but pompous and stiff. "Look, I'm really not interested."

"I'm sorry," he said. "I don't mean to intrude, but if I can do anything to help solve your problem or make you happy, I would consider it an honor."

Alyssa felt herself soften.   Just because you miss José doesn't mean that you can't be nice. She placed her hand on his arm. "You're right, I've not been happy. My name is Alyssa. Take me for coffee and I'll tell you about it."

They ordered *espressos*. "I saw you tracing the name 'José' on your notebook," Diego said.

"José is my cousin. Everyone calls him, 'Amigo' because he's a good friend to everybody. He was accepted into the Naval Academy and now I never get to see him. His studies and naval exercises take up all his time. We're like a brother and a sister. Maybe we're even closer than a brother and a sister. I'm sick with missing him."

"I thought it might be the name of a boyfriend."

"No, I've never had a boyfriend."

Diego relaxed. The name this beautiful girl had been tracing was not a boyfriend. She'd never had one. It gave him confidence. He wouldn't be competing with someone else or with the memory of someone else. "Your cousin is very lucky to have such a beautiful and intelligent woman thinking about him."

"What makes you think I'm intelligent?"

"There are very few women at the university and you're the only girl in the Physics class. You must not only be very smart, but independent, also."

"Perhaps I am."

"Tell me about your cousin."

Alyssa smiled. "He's very smart. He's not very big, but he's a fine athlete. Our mothers were sisters, but his mother died when we were young. His father's a mechanic and never had the resources to give José any extras, so he spent a lot of time with my family. We basically grew up together."

"What does your father do?" Dicgo said.

"My father is Colonel Hernando Villanueva."

"Ah, yes, I've heard of him. He's a powerful man," Diego said.

"And what about you, Diego, what do you want to be?"

"I want to be a lawyer. I'm very ambitious."

Alyssa studied the 'ambitious' young man seated across from her. He impressed her as pompous and arrogant and very full of himself. But with José gone, there was no one in whom she could confide. At least, Diego would be someone she could talk to.

14

José and Roberto sat on the dock in front of *Criollo,* enjoying the warmth of the afternoon sun. They'd just finished washing the boat down after a training run.

"Sixty-seven feet of varnished mahogany with teak decks. Have you ever seen anything so beautiful, Amigo?"

"She's very beautiful, Macho, especially under sail. I can't wait to race on her to St. Petersburg."

"Me, too. We're going to learn a lot from Oliva. He's been taking care of her since she was made in the Canary Islands. It's gonna be great!"

"You know, Macho," José said, "I think it's time you met my cousin."

"You have a cousin?"

""*Sí,* our mothers escaped the Nazis just before the war."

"The Nazis?"

"*Sí,* my grandfather got them out of Poland just before Hitler invaded. My mother got sick on the trip and never fully recovered. She died not long after I was born."

"What does your cousin look like?"

"I tell you the truth, Macho, she's gorgeous beyond belief."

"So, why haven't you told me about her before?"

"Because Alyssa is special. She's the best girl in the world." José put his hands up in anticipation of Roberto's doubt. "No, no, Roberto, the *best*. The very *best*. She's smart, she's funny and she has the best heart God ever put inside a woman. She's a no-bullshit person."

"*And* she's beautiful?"

"*Sí*, she's *very* beautiful."

Roberto laughed. "C'mon, Amigo, if she's your cousin, how good looking can she really be?"

José bounced a wet sponge off Roberto's face.

15

"But, Amigo," Alyssa said, when José called to tell her about Roberto and the conversation they'd had. "I've started seeing someone I met here at school."

"No! Don't tell me this, Alyssa. You've never been interested in *any* man before. You always say none of them ever hold any attraction for you…that you have more important things to occupy your time."

"I know, Amigo. But it's different now that you're not around to keep me company."

"So, who is this guy, anyway? What do you know about him and how do you know he can be trusted?"

"He's a very respectable person and he comes from a good family."

"Are you in love with him?"

"No, not yet anyway. But, so far, he's been nice."

"If you're not in love with him, then drop him. Trust me, Alyssa, my friend is the man for you. He's strong and handsome…during the physical tests for the academy, he was the most impressive. He also got very high scores on the academic tests. You must believe me, my cousin. God made you and Macho for each other."

"Macho?" Alyssa said. "My God, Amigo. Do you really think I'd be interested in someone with such a name?"

"It's just a family nickname that he's had since he was a boy. I've gotten to know him well and I've seen that he's an honorable person. But I tell you, little cousin, he's much more even than that—it's your destiny to fall in love with him."

"Well, you do sound pretty convinced about this. I guess it would be alright to at least meet him. Nobody knows me as well as you do, Amigo."

"Good," José said. "Then it's settled. We'll come to visit over the holidays."

Alyssa, sighed. "Alright, I'll tell my parents you'll be coming. They'll be excited to see you."

"Okay, it's all set," José told Roberto. "Alyssa's expecting us, and my father said we can use his car. It's a 1955 Pontiac convertible—red with red leather interior. We'll be the kings of Havana!"

"That's great, Amigo! We'll have to fight the girls off!"

"*I'll* have to fight the girls off, Macho. You will have a girl. The *best* girl."

Roberto sighed. "*Sí*, Amigo. *Sí*."

"First, I'll go home and spend a couple of days with my father," José said. "Then I'll drive the car to your house and pick you up and we'll go see Alyssa."

"Okay, but I'd like for you to meet my family, too," Roberto said. "We could spend a couple of days there before we go to Havana. Bring your father. I'm sure he and my father would get along great and my mother loves having company to cook for. You haven't lived until you've tasted her *ropa vieja*. My father just bought a boat. Maybe we can do some fishing."

"That would be cool, Macho. My father loves to fish. This vacation is going to be great!"

16

The Valiente family spilled out of the house when they heard the horn of the red convertible. "Hey, Macho!" José leaped from the car without opening the door.

"Amigo!" They embraced and made introductions. "This is my father, my mother, my sister, Maria, her husband, and my uncle, Tomo."

"And this is my father, Enrique," José said.

"*Mucho gusto*," Enrique said. He and Roberto embraced, and the two older men shook hands.

Ernesto nodded at the grease-stained hand of the mechanic, which he gripped in his own tobacco-stained hand. "I guess there's no hiding the evidence of our trades, eh Enrique?" he said.

Enrique smiled. "No," he said, "our hands are honest."

"*Bienvenido*, welcome to our home."

"*Muchas gracias*, it's very kind of you to invite us."

Violetta clapped her hands. "Come in, come in! The *ropa vieja* has been cooking all day. I'm so happy to have people in my house, especially the good friend of Roberto from the Naval Academy and his father. Dinner is waiting for you!"

"First, we should have a drink," Ernesto said, "to celebrate this meeting."

"That reminds me," Enrique said, "we brought some wine." He retrieved two bottles of *rioja* from the back seat of the car. They led the party into the house, their arms around each other's shoulders.

They finished the two bottles of *Rioja* Enrique brought, consumed all the *ropa vieja* and started on another bottle Ernesto placed on the table. "I have an idea," he said. "I think we should take my boat out fishing, tomorrow. She's not much to look at, but she's solid and seaworthy and the engine runs good."

"Good idea, Papi," Roberto said. "What do you think, José? Do you and your father want to go?"

"Definitely!" José said. Enrique nodded.

"I've always wanted to see *Isla Paraiso*," Ernesto said. "I've heard it's truly a paradise and that the fishing there is excellent. If we left early in the morning, we could make it up there, do some fishing and be back before dark."

"Papi," Violetta said, "isn't that a long way to go in a boat you've only taken in and out of the harbor a couple of times?"

"She's a fine boat," Ernesto said. "She looks a little rough, but I have faith in her. Besides, if the motor gives out, she has a sail that can get us home safely."

Violetta sighed. The men were caught up in the idea of this boat trip. They all talked at once about the equipment they would take, the bait they would use and the fish they would catch. There was no stopping them now. She looked across the table to Maria.

Maria nodded at the wine bottle and shrugged. The result had been inevitable.

17

Dawn was breaking when they arrived at the harbor in Enrique's car and filed down to the dock. Only Tomo had escaped a hangover. Despite their discomfort, no one suggested that they not go. No matter how miserable they felt, they were committed.

Approaching Ernesto's boat, each man made his own private estimate of the vessel's chances. She was twenty-five feet long with a small cabin and two berths. Once white, the paint that remained had yellowed. In many places weathered gray wood was visible where paint had blistered and peeled away. José tried to read the name on the stern. It was faded and chipped, but enough remained that he was able to piece it together… "*Mojito.*"

Ernesto turned the key and pushed the start button. The engine coughed into life. The exhaust smoked heavily at first, but gradually cleared. He smiled. "All she needs is a little paint. Come aboard, my friends. Let's go fishing."

They climbed down into the boat and stowed their fishing gear, extra clothing, lunches, and the cooler of beer. Roberto and José cast off the lines and they motored out into Havana harbor.

Tomo had never been in a boat before, so he stood close to Ernesto at the wheel and stared straight ahead. The harbor was quiet as the boat chugged through it, past the old fort, El Morro, which guarded the entrance and on out into the Straits of Florida. After they cleared the channel and entered deep water, Ernesto changed their course to the west. For a while they were accompanied by a few commercial fishing boats, which were also getting an early start on the day. But soon the fishing boats turned away and they were alone on the water.

"How will we find this little island out here in the middle of all this water?" said Enrique.

"Take the wheel, Machito," Ernesto said. He spread a chart over the engine box in the middle of the boat. "Look here, Enrique. This is Isla Paraiso here and we're here, near the mouth of the harbor. You can see it's just a little south of due west. So, our heading will be 265 degrees, which we'll follow using the compass mounted in front of the steering post. We'll find the island by dead reckoning, following our course and figuring that the effects of winds and currents will average out. At fifteen miles per hour, it should take us around three hours. At noon, we should all start keeping a sharp eye out for it."

They took turns napping in the two bunks on either side of the cabin, sleeping away the wine from the night before. Ernesto and Enrique were together on deck while the others slept, below. "I'm enjoying getting to know you, Enrique," Ernesto said. "But I like to talk politics, and I know nothing about your views. Me, I'm a socialist…from each according to his ability, to each according to his needs. That's what I believe."

"You're kidding yourself, Macho. Nothing's ever going to change in Cuba."

"Batista won't be in power forever, Enrique. We must be ready when he's done."

Enrique sighed. "In the few years I had with my wife before she died, she taught me a lot about people and the world beyond our shores. She was very smart, Macho, so before you get started, allow me to share some of her wisdom with you. Political arguments are a waste of time. Everyone's passionate about their opinions, but nobody really knows what they're talking about. People want to appear sophisticated and knowledgeable and act as though they have everything all figured out, but they don't research the issues beyond what it takes to support the positions they already hold. When the arguing is done, all that's been proven is that they disagree. Everyone's political beliefs are profoundly pathetic and ill-founded, except of course for mine," he chuckled, "which are God-given and divinely inspired. So, while I haven't known you very long, Macho, I treasure our friendship and have come to love you like a brother. Please, my friend, let's enjoy our time together and don't tarnish the respect I have for you by trotting your political philosophy out in front of me."

Ernesto opened his mouth to speak but thought better of it. He only shook his head and turned back to the wheel.

At 10:30, Roberto was awakened by Tomo. "Machito, Papi wants you to come up."

"Take the helm, Machito," Ernesto said when Roberto climbed up to the cockpit. "Keep the course at 265 degrees. We want to stay between the reefs and the Gulf Stream. I'm going down and take a nap, myself. Have Tomo wake me in a half-hour. We should be getting close by then."

"*Sí*, Papi."

The wheel felt good in Roberto's hands and the wooden deck felt solid and warm beneath his bare feet. Except for the regular swells, the water was nearly flat. He spread his feet wide to balance himself against the soft rolling of the boat. So far, there were no reefs in sight. He focused his attention on the compass. The 265-degree mark on the compass bobbed back and forth behind the indicator.

A white wake spread out behind them. Tomo developed a fascination with the wake. He sat on the back of the engine box and watched it for long periods. There was little else to look at, except the coastline of Cuba receding into the distance.

Enrique stood next to Roberto. "I looked under the box," he said. "It's a Grey Marine engine. Six cylinders. A Grey Marine is a good motor."

"That's good to hear," Roberto said. "I think we're almost there, but we've got a long trip back."

"It's very beautiful and peaceful out here," Enrique said.

"Yes," Roberto said.

"It's nice to get away from land for a while."

"Do you get tired of working on cars?"

"No, I love working on the cars. It's my passion. I like making things work the way they should. The world, it doesn't always work the way it should. People make it that way. I have no control over that. The machines, the engines, those I can control. I can make them run smoothly. It's very enjoyable for me."

"That's good," Roberto said.

"Do you like the academy?"

"Very much. We're learning a lot."

"I understand that you and José will be sailing to the U.S."

"Yes, I'm looking forward to that."

"I've always wanted to go to the United States," Enrique said. "They have lots of cars."

"We'll tell you all about it when we get back."

"I wish I could go."

"We could stow you away below decks," Roberto said.

Enrique laughed. "Don't tempt me, Machito. I might do it. Someday I'll go. José and I will go together after he graduates from the academy. We haven't spent enough time together. That's the way it is sometimes. Everyone does the best they can. Some things, we cannot control."

"It's almost 11:30," Roberto said. "Tomo, it's time to wake Papi."

"*Sí*," Tomo said. He left his post on the back of the engine box and moved toward the cabin. "I must wake Papi."

Ernesto and José came up on deck. José looked around. "I don't see anything."

"Everyone, keep a sharp lookout," Ernesto said. "The island's very small. I've been told only two families live on it. The first one to see *Isla Paraiso* gets to open the first beer."

Roberto looked around. "Beer sounds good, but what I really would like is some water."

"Damn!" Ernesto slammed his fist on the gunwale. "I knew we forgot something! We'd better find that island."

Twenty minutes later, José pointed to the horizon, "I think I see something! Look, just a little to the left! Yes, there it is! I see it!"

"Yes," Ernesto said. "I see it, too." He adjusted their course to line up with the speck on the horizon. The speck grew larger, and trees became visible. "Yes, that must be it. I knew the *Mojito* could make it."

The island was encircled by reefs. They circled it twice before they saw the little white buoy marking the channel entrance. They wound their way through the channel to the southern side of the island, where they found a small, protected landing.

An old man appeared on the dock. He caught the dock line they threw to him and smiled shyly. "Do you have any fresh water," Ernesto asked him.

"Yes, we have fresh water. I'll go up and get you some."

"I'll go with you," Roberto said. "I'd like to stretch my legs."

They walked together up the path. A small woman with a big smile displaying perfect white teeth stood in the neat yard of the house. "*Hola*," she said. "*Bienvinedo*, welcome."

"I'm Paco and this is my wife, Lena," the man said.

"My pleasure, *señora*."

The woman reached up and hugged Roberto around the neck. She kissed him on both cheeks and then stepped back and smiled shyly. "Welcome to Isla Paraiso."

"Thank you. Your island's very pretty." So strange, Roberto thought. How did people come to live in such a place?

The three of them walked back down to the boat with two jars of water. "Why do you live way out here?" Roberto asked. "You're so far away from everything."

"We're not far from everything," Paco said. "Everything is far from here. I fish. Lena works in her garden. We're very happy." Lena nodded. The big smile never seemed to fade from her little face. "The best fishing is along the outside of the reef on this side of the island. The big fish come up from the deep water to get the little fish that go too far away from the safety of the rocks."

"*Muchas gracias*," Roberto said, "we're in your debt."

"We're happy we were able to help you," Paco said.

Lena hugged him and again kissed him on both cheeks. "Come see us again, someday."

Roberto saw tears in the corners of her eyes when he pulled away to return to the boat. What strange little people. "I just might," he said.

The men motored out to where Pqco had suggested and caught enough fish to fill the cooler. They laughed and joked, drank beer and fished until the afternoon had passed. On the trip home, the currents ran against them. The day had faded into darkness when they saw the lights of Havana Harbor. Violetta and Maria were waiting on the dock when they arrived. "*Dios mio*," Violetta said. "We were worried about you."

Ernesto wrapped her in an embrace. Then he walked up the dock with one arm around the shoulders of Violetta and the other around the shoulders of Enrique. "We filled the cooler with fish and had a fine time. Enrique and I are brothers."

18

Alyssa awoke feeling uneasy. This was the day José was bringing his friend to their house. He said they were "made for each other." She lay in bed thinking about José's description of the man and what meeting him would be like. An unfamiliar emotion washed over her, and anxious thoughts raced through her head. What if he doesn't like me? Which dress? Which shoes? Put my hair up or leave it down? "Alyssa, please—what is wrong with you? Get control of yourself! Stop thinking like this before you make yourself crazy. Go out and do something else for a while."

She dressed and went downstairs. Juliana was in the kitchen making preparations for dinner. Alyssa kissed her cheek. "What are you making, Mami?"

"*Paella*—José's favorite. You remember he's coming today and bringing his friend? They'll be here at noon."

Alyssa sighed. "*Sí*, Mami, I remember." She hadn't shared with her mother the conversation she'd had with José about his friend. Juliana excited easily. Telling her José thought she and this man were destined would have made her impossible. She moved toward the door to the garage.

"Where're you going?" Juliana said.

"I think I'll go for a ride on my bicycle."

"Your bicycle? Why? You haven't ridden your bicycle in years."

"*Sí*, Mami, I know," Alyssa said. "I just feel like getting a little exercise."

Juliana watched her leave. She continued to stare at the doorway after Alyssa had gone. In her hand she held the *langostino* she'd been cleaning. Her mouth hung slightly open, as though there was more she wanted to say.

The bicycle's tires were flat when Alyssa dragged it from a corner of the garage, but they pumped up without complaint and she rode toward the sea. Fresh air was what she needed and being on the bicycle was good therapy. The rhythmic pumping of the pedals helped her to feel like herself again.

She rode to El Morro. From atop its walls, she could look out over the Straits of Florida. The sea below was a windswept patchwork of blues and greens stretching out to the deeper blue of the Gulf Stream. Alyssa spread her arms and inhaled the cool salt air. White wisps of clouds streaked the sky.

An old woman dressed in black watched her from a nearby bench. When Alyssa noticed her, the woman smiled and nodded at the clouds. "Horsetails," she said. "A change in the weather is coming."

Alyssa sat on the edge of the wall and thought about José and the friend she was going to meet today. What if José was right and this guy turned out to be…what…the love of her life? The improbability both amused and excited her. She wondered why she'd never dreamed of, or even hoped for, something like that before. Most girls did, didn't they? It's what they usually talked about. There always seemed to be some guy they had their hopes pinned on. The scope and prospect of their lives was wrapped up in getting married. "What about that, Alyssa?" she asked herself. "Why is it that you're not on that quest? Is there something wrong with *you*? Ha! No, I think I just have a stronger sense of myself than most and this friend of José's will really need to be something if I'm going to give *that* up!"

She sat looking out to sea a little longer and finished her time on the wall with a long sigh. You can't stay out here forever. You'd better go see what this is all about. She looked at her watch…it was later than she thought. She ran down the steps and out of El Morro. She wheeled her bike to the pavement, but the tires were flat, again! She pumped them up with the little hand pump on the bike, but they kept losing air on the way home and every few minutes she had to stop and pump them up again.

Roberto slept late. The long boat trip had exhausted him, but when he rose, he felt strong and calm. It was the same calm he remembered feeling when he stepped to the plate in a tight baseball game. Nothing existed during those moments but him and the ball. Everything else disappeared. He didn't hear the cheering of fans or teammates. There wasn't even a pitcher. There was only the ball. Stepping to the plate was like entering a dream…everything slowed down. Today he would meet José's cousin. Are you ready for this, Roberto? For better or worse, he was ready.

José and Roberto dropped Enrique and continued to the Villanueva's house in the convertible. "I've been waiting for this day," José said.

"So have I," Roberto said. "I want to meet this cousin of yours."

"You really don't know what you're in for do you, my friend?"

"What are you saying, Amigo? You've always talked reverently about your cousin and predicted only glorious success for our relationship. Now, we're on our way to her house and you're telling me something different?"

"No," José said. "I'm not saying anything different. I just want you to think of the most amazing girl you've ever known. No, think of the most amazing girl you've ever *dreamed* of. You have the image? Okay, now double it. That's Alyssa."

"Oh," Roberto said. "Okay. You're right, I don't know what I'm 'in for,' but whatever it is, I'm looking forward to it."

They entered a wealthy section of Havana. "Welcome to Cubanacan," José said.

Roberto looked around them. He'd had no idea there were so many rich people.

José turned into a circular drive that curved in front of a large, two-story house. Roberto tried to not look impressed. It was one thing to drive through an affluent neighborhood but pulling up in front of one of the largest houses as a guest was overwhelming.

Juliana and Colonel Villanueva came out of the house to greet them. "José, José, it's been so long since we've seen you!" Juliana cried. They were wearing their white cadet uniforms, and she stepped back to look at them. "You both look so beautiful." She put her hands to her mouth in the way some women do when it seems they might break into tears.

"Beautiful car," the colonel said.

"It's my father's," José said. "He's letting us use it during the break. Roberto, meet Colonel and *señora* Villanueva, my aunt and uncle. At the academy, we just call him 'Macho'."

Juliana put her arms around Roberto and gave him a quick kiss on the cheek. He and the colonel shook hands. "Welcome to our home."

"*Gracias*," Roberto said. "It's kind of you to invite me. José has told me much about you both."

"It's too bad our daughter, Alyssa, isn't here," Juliana said.

"What?" José said.

"She left on her bicycle a couple of hours ago and hasn't returned. I thought she'd be back by now. It's been a long time since she's ridden a bicycle. I hope she hasn't fallen or forgotten how to use the brakes."

José laughed. "Alyssa will be fine." He put his arm around Juliana and led her toward the house. "My aunt worries too much," he said over his shoulder to Roberto.

Colonel Villanueva gestured Roberto ahead of him. He impressed Roberto with his traditional bearing and manners. Roberto was also impressed with the interior of the house. He'd never been inside a house like this. Everything looked expensive. Despite his desire to appear casual, he couldn't resist taking a quick look around and above him when they entered. The ceiling seemed to go up forever. The floors were magnificently tiled and so polished that it appeared you might slip if you stepped too quickly. The heavy furniture and the paintings on the walls made it feel more like being in a museum than in a home.

Juliana led them into a room where a sofa and two chairs surrounded a low marble table. At one end of the room was a bar. "Would anyone care for a drink?" said the colonel.

"*Sí*," José said.

"*Mojitos*?" asked the colonel.

"*Sí, por favor*!" said José. "Macho, you must have one of my uncle's *Mojitos*. Take it from me, they're the best in Cuba."

Roberto had heard of these drinks, but never had one. Colonel Villanueva crushed limes into juice, mixed in sugar and rum then dropped in ice and finished with a sprig of mint.

Roberto took a sip of his drink and smiled. "Excellent."

Juliana took a seat across from Roberto. What a handsome young man was this friend of José's…so well-mannered and intelligent. "I wish Alyssa would get back here."

They'd settled with their drinks and José had begun telling the Villanuevas about their experiences at the academy when they heard the front door fly open.

She'd planned to be home by noon, but constant stopping to pump up the bicycle's tires made it nearly one o'clock before Alyssa reached the house. The red convertible of José's father was parked in the driveway.

She dropped the bike on the lawn. The exertions had her heart pounding. She pushed the door handle too forcefully, and it flung open. This was not the way she'd wanted to meet José's friend. She was breathing hard and knew she must look flushed. Her hair was in disarray and her clothes were damp with perspiration. Moisture was visible across her brow and glistened on her arms and legs. She pushed at her hair, but it was of little use.

Running upstairs to arrange herself would only take more time…she'd just make the best of it.

José and his friend set their drinks down and rose from the sofa when Alyssa entered the room. She smiled at her parents and José, but her eyes locked onto those of the handsome stranger in the white uniform.

When they heard the front door open, Roberto felt his pulse begin to race. And then…she was there…the cousin José had talked about so much. Her chest rose and fell as she tried to catch her breath—her smile was stunning, and she looked right at him. Roberto stared back at her. His body felt heavy and immovable. José was right, she was spectacular. Her tousled hair was dark and thick and fell to her shoulders. Her body was tanned and athletic. He watched as José embraced her, then knew he was being introduced but heard nothing. Vision was the only one of his senses that seemed to be working. She had penetrating brown eyes that never left his, even as she returned José's embrace.

Her parents occupied the two chairs, so the only place for Alyssa to sit was on the sofa between José and Roberto. Roberto could feel the damp heat emanating from her body. Her smell was intoxicating.

Colonel Villanueva went to the bar to make more *Mojitos*. Alyssa could hear conversation taking place. She heard herself saying things but didn't know what they were—her voice seemed to belong to someone else. She tried to avoid staring at Roberto, but her glance was drawn in his direction at every opportunity.

After a second *Mojito*, she excused herself and went upstairs to change for dinner. She sat on a cushion and brushed her hair in the mirror. "What's happening to me?" Her body felt thrilled, like when her father had pushed her up high on a swing as a little girl. But this feeling wasn't going away—it was a constant elation. The exhilaration felt wonderful, but a rivulet of dread trickled through her—was she was losing control of herself? "What about me? Am I losing me?"

She debated about what she should wear. She tried on three different dresses, before she finally sat down on the bed and took a deep breath. "What are you doing, Alyssa?" She'd been preparing to pick from among her shoes, but now slipped on the first pair of flats she found and left the bedroom. "You are who you are…get on with it."

She joined her mother in the kitchen. "Where's Berta?"

"I told her to take the day off," Juliana said. "I wanted to do this myself and she makes me crazy trying to help."

"And grandma and grandpa...are they coming?"

Juliana looked out the kitchen window and nodded. "They're coming up the walk, now."

"Is there anything I can do for you?"

Juliana was layering the bottom of the serving dish with yellow rice. She ignored Alyssa's offer of assistance. "So, you like this young man?" she asked quietly.

Alyssa turned away and walked to the window. "I think so." Her mother had stopped trying to match her up with boys, years ago. This was the first conversation they'd had about men in a long time. "Do you like him, Mami?"

"*Sí*, I like him very much. I can see why he and José have become such good friends. And so handsome!" Juliana poured steaming seafood stew over the rice until it filled the dish, then placed six large *langostinos* in a circle around the top. The shrimp were plump and pink, and the dish looked beautiful. "Seeing you sitting next to Roberto made me feel very happy."

"I'm all caught up in my emotions, Mami. I don't know how I should act or what I should say. I'm starting to feel like I don't even know who I am. I think it's the first time in my life that I'm not sure of myself."

"Don't worry, my dear, everything will be fine. I can see that he likes you, too. Now, get out of here. Go and tell the men the *paella* is ready before you make me start crying."

The colonel and Juliana sat at opposite ends of the dining table. Alyssa sat on one side with her grandparents. The two cadets sat across from her. She made introductions. "Roberto, these are my grandparents. My grandmother only speaks Polish. They escaped the Nazis with my mother and my aunt just before World War II started. My grandfather's a psychiatrist."

Juliana put her hand on Isaak's. "It took us forever on the trains to Lisbon and then forever on the boat to Cuba, but we made it, didn't we, papa?"

Isaak smiled and nodded. "Just in time, too. When we arrived here, we were told that Hitler had invaded Poland while we were on the boat. We were lucky."

José carried most of the conversation, which included the story of their boat trip to *Isla Paraiso*. Several times Roberto and Alyssa caught each other's glances and exchanged embarrassed smiles.

"You're from Santa Fe?" Juliana said. "We used to summer there. Have you ever seen a rogue wave?"

"I've heard of them, but I've never seen one," Roberto said.

"When Alyssa was a little girl, she was swept from the beach by a big wave at Santa Fe. It would have drowned her, but she was rescued by an army sergeant."

"His name was Gomez," the colonel said. "I agreed to recommend him for the military academy out of gratitude."

"Did he make it?"

"He did. He graduated from the academy and is now an officer." Colonel Villanueva didn't mention the treasure he'd been keeping a secret for so many years. He said nothing about it being hidden in this very house, waiting for a government that could be trusted to share the treasure with its people.

"I think I remember Sargeant Gomez," Roberto said. "Once when I was little, I was fishing for shrimp with my sister and my uncle when we stumbled upon an old pipe. My father cut the pipe open and found a treasure map inside. He was digging for the treasure when Sergeant Gomez stopped him. He told my father that any treasure would belong to the government, but that my father would receive a reward if anything was ever found."

"Treasure! Like pirate's treasure?" Juliana said. "My goodness, how exciting! Did they find anything?"

"I guess not," Roberto said. "It was all just a fantasy." Colonel Villanueva nearly choked on his *paella* when Roberto told his story but continued his meal in silence.

After dinner, they moved to the veranda overlooking the gardens at the rear of the house. Colonel Villanueva offered cigars to Isaak, Roberto and José and the men smoked.

"I think Roberto might enjoy seeing the neighborhood by evening. Why don't you give him a tour, Alyssa?" José said.

Roberto nodded. "I'd like that,"

Alyssa felt her face flush. "Okay, let's go."

All during dinner, Roberto had absorbed Alyssa's beauty. The shape of her lips, the texture of her skin, and her eyes with the light from the dinner candles dancing in them. He had wanted to reach across the table and caress her cheek. Now, as they strolled through the streets of the neighborhood, he reached for her hand. She didn't withdraw. The contact was firm and warm and seemed like it had always been there, waiting to be discovered…like a buried treasure.

When Roberto slipped his hand over hers, Alyssa was surprised at how comfortable it felt. Their fingers interlaced. It all seemed so natural. Could this be love she was feeling? Everyone said it was hard, but this seemed so easy and uncomplicated. "Well, I guess there is *one* complication," she thought.

Roberto's desire overwhelmed him. He stopped walking and pulled Alyssa to him. His eyes were filled with passion and his lips sought hers. She pulled back and placed a hand against his chest. "Not yet, Roberto. I cannot. I want to, but first I must explain all this to someone else."

19

February 1958

Roberto and José stood on the walls of El Morro and watched the Southern Ocean Racing Conference yachts stream into Havana Harbor. Roberto pointed to a sleek ketch sailing fast through the light chop of the waves. "See that big one in front? That's *Finisterre*. She won the SORC championship in 1956."

Nearly a hundred boats stretched out behind *Finisterre*, as they raced down to Havana from Miami. "I see her," José said. "She's magnificent! Do you think we can beat her?"

"I don't know, she looks pretty fast. But we have the secret weapon, Amigo," Roberto said. "Oliva."

"*Sí*, we have Oliva!" José said. "Look at that big guy standing in front of the mast on *Finisterre*." A red-haired man loomed large on the foredeck of the big ketch. He had one hand on the mast and his legs spread wide, as *Finisterre* crossed the finish line beneath the shadow of El Morro. The man had been watching the tell-tails of the genoa sail. As the boat crossed in front of the fort, he glanced up and saw them. He waved and raised one hand high with his thumb sticking up.

They waved back and returned his sign of triumph. "We'll be the ones standing on the foredeck and signaling victory when we sail first into St. Petersburg," José said. "I'm so excited I don't know if I can sleep the next two nights before we take off."

"You think you're excited?" Roberto said. "Have you talked to Carlos lately? He hasn't pooped in four days."

José laughed. "That's not from excitement, that's from fear. He knows he's going to be seasick the whole trip."

The two cadets escorted Alyssa up the steps of the Havana Yacht Club, one on each arm. Heads turned to watch the striking woman in a strapless black dress enter the club. She no longer fought the feelings she'd been experiencing since meeting Roberto. She wasn't sure if it was love, but she liked it.

Diego hadn't taken their breakup well. The intensity of his anger surprised her. His parting words conveyed a bitter, threatening tone. "Things are changing in Cuba, Alyssa. You may soon find yourself very sorry that you did this to me!"

Alyssa hadn't told Diego the identity of her new boyfriend, but when she told Roberto about the breakup scene, he recognized the name of Diego Montalvo, the son of the man who ran the cigar factory where his father worked. "I know, Diego, and we have not been friends," he said to Alyssa. "If he ever finds out that it's me you left him for, he'll be even more upset."

The party was jumping when the three of them arrived. Rum flowed and hot Latin rhythms pulsed through the club. White-clothed tables encircled the dance floor. José pointed to an unoccupied table. "The crews really enjoy coming to Cuba," he said. "Our parties are legendary among the SORC fleet. They'll be dancing all night."

Roberto looked around the room. "There're going to be some sailors with big headaches racing to St. Petersburg, tomorrow."

Carlos staggered over. "Great party!" he shouted over the sound of the band. "Free rum!" He brandished a glass over his head.

"Has he gone yet?" Roberto said, after Carlos moved on to another table.

"I don't think so," José said.

Alyssa looked from one to the other. "What do you mean, 'has he gone yet'?"

"Carlos has been having some trouble with his digestive system," José said. "It's been a full week since he's been able to defecate."

"And he's sailing to Florida tomorrow? That's insane!"

"It is insane," José said. "Maybe the alcohol will loosen him up a bit."

"It could make things worse."

Roberto rose from the table. "I'll get some drinks. Bacardi and Coke?"

Alyssa and José both nodded.

The area around the bar was crowded. Roberto squeezed through, until he stood with his elbows on the bar. As he waited for the attention of one of the busy bartenders, someone jostled in next to him. Roberto recognized the big red-haired man who'd waved to them from the deck of *Finisterre,* beneath El Morro. The man appeared even larger in person. He was a full head taller than Roberto. Above the waist, he was built like an oil drum.

"Sorry," the man said, "tight quarters." The club was hot, and he was perspiring heavily. The armpits of his blue yachting blazer were stained with sweat. "*Finisterre*" was stitched in gold letters across one breast pocket. The man smiled and offered his hand. "My name's Chip…Chip Magner."

"Roberto Valiente." He shook the beefy hand of the big man. "We saw you on the foredeck when you entered the harbor. You waved to us up on El Morro."

"That was you standing up there? You guys must have had a great view."

"Yes, it looked like you were going very fast."

"We've been tearing up the SORC for the past few years," Magner said.

"Is it your boat?"

"Yep. She's an exceptional boat and I have a great crew." Magner took note of Roberto's uniform. "But I hear you young Cubans may have something special in store for us."

"How do you know about us?" Roberto said.

Magner grinned. "We do our homework."

"You speak Spanish very well."

"My mother's Puerto Rican," Magner said. "I grew up speaking Spanish, although I'm from Brooklyn, New York. My father's Irish, but when I talk with my mother, it's always in Spanish. You've heard of Brooklyn?"

"*Sí*," Roberto said. "The Brooklyn Dodgers are there."

Magner frowned. "They *used* to be there," he said.

"How is it that you're able to spend so much time racing sailboats? The SORC lasts all winter, doesn't it?"

"I'm in the import/export business," Magner said. "Most of my business is with Central and South American companies. The key is assembling a competent management staff. Things run smoothly, even when I'm not there. But let's talk about racing. Do you think your Canary Island yawl can beat my Rhode Island-built Hereshoff ketch?"

"Maybe," Roberto said. "We have a secret weapon."

"The *Canario*? Yes, I've heard about him, too."

"You even know about Oliva? How do you know these things?"

"Of course, we know about him. Homework, *amigo*," Magner said, "homework."

"The *Criollo*'s a great boat," Roberto said. "We're inexperienced, but we've been training hard for months. Under Oliva's hand and with a little luck, we might be able to beat you."

"Okay," Magner said. "What do you say we put something on it…loser buys the winner a drink when we reach St. Pete?"

"You're on."

"*Buena suerte*," Magner said, "we'll see you in St. Pete."

Roberto placed the drinks in front of Alyssa and José. "Guess who I was just talking to—the big red-haired guy we saw on the deck of *Finisterre*. We made a bet on who would get to St. Petersburg first."

José raised his glass. "It will be *Criollo*!"

"To *Criollo*," Roberto said. "The guy's name is Magner. He knows *Criollo* was built in the Canary Islands, he knows about Oliva, and he speaks Spanish."

"He just sails around all the time?" Alyssa said. "How can he do that?"

"He said he owns an international import/export business that does a lot of business in Central and South America."

Alyssa laughed. "Maybe, he's a spy!"

Roberto smiled. José's marvelous cousin was radiant and delicious, and he wouldn't be seeing her again until they returned from the United States in a week. She tossed her hair back as she laughed and the expanse of tanned skin from her neck down to her strapless evening gown made Roberto want to leap across the table and bury his face in the small of her throat.

The sun was beginning to warm the morning as the boats tacked back and forth behind the starting line. A big ketch glided up next to them…*Finisterre*. Chip Magner grinned at them from his place at the wheel. He saw Roberto and made a drinking motion with one hand. "*Buena suerte!*" he called. "See you in St. Pete!"

Roberto waved. "*Buena suerte, señor* Magner!"

A feeling of race-day excitement charged the air. Roberto moved near Carlos, who was looking more pale than ever. "You, okay?"

Carlos grimaced. "I'll be alright, I just wish we'd get started,"

Roberto looked at his watch. "It won't be long now. Have you gone yet?"

"Not yet."

Criollo had her spinnaker up and had been sailing well for several hours. It was nearly midnight when the strong wind gusts began. With each gust, *Criollo* surged ahead, rocking first to one side and then the other.

A flash of lightning lit the area around them. For a moment, across the whitecaps, they could see *Finisterre* just ahead of them. Men could be seen scrambling on her deck. José moved up to the bow for a better look. *"Finisterre's* dropping her spinnaker!"

Criollo began to heave violently from side to side, trying to spill the wind from the big sail. Her spinnaker pole scraped the surface of the water each time she rolled to starboard. Oliva rushed up on deck and grabbed the wheel. "Drop the spinnaker! Drop it now! We're caught in a death roll!" The cadets struggled to keep their footing on the steep and slippery decks. As the boat buried her rub rails, they clung to anything within reach.

"We can't get the spinnaker in!" José shouted. "The wind's too strong!"

"Cut the spinnaker lines! Cut the lines or we're going over!"

Rain beat down upon them. With one final heave *Criollo* swung around parallel to the waves, trying to put her nose into the wind.

They hadn't felt the full force of the storm when they were running before it, but when the boat turned broadside to its path, the wind intensified, whipping across the water, and whistling through the rigging. A gust caught the back of the mainsail and threw *Criollo* onto her side, pinning her against the water.

With the pressure on the back of the mainsail released, the wind and waves gradually turned the boat into the wind and *Criollo* rose upright, again. "Now get rid of that damn spinnaker," Oliva said. "Everybody okay?"

They were all shaken, but Carlos returned from a trip to the head, smiling broadly. Rain pelted his face as he raised his arms to the sky and began to dance.

"Get that jib up," Oliva said. "We have a race to win."

20

"Captain Gomez, I want you to take your men up into the Sierra Maestra Mountains. Track down the bandit, Castro, and kill him."

Finally, something important…satisfaction spread through Gomez. His superiors recognized his potential. Being sent after Castro was a great honor. The bandit's reputation was formidable…many others had tried and failed. But hadn't he graduated near the head of his class at the *Academia Militar*? And now he'd reached the rank of Captain. Of course, there were others who'd been more successful, but they had familial advantages and connections to upper-level authority. Gomez's accomplishments had been made through hard work and recognizing opportunity when he saw it.

He'd found that working one's way through the elite wasn't all that difficult. It was simple, really. Begin by finding someone who has connections. Once they believe they have your undivided loyalty and support, they begin to depend upon you. They know you don't have any connections of your own, so you can't betray them. As they advance, they must take you with them. They need someone they can trust…their enemies are everywhere. And now this opportunity.

"Some years ago," the general said, "Castro was caught and jailed for attacking the Moncada Army Barracks in Santiago de Cuba. After a couple years in jail, he was released and exiled to Mexico, but he wasn't finished. He had the balls to invade Cuba with only 80 men in December of 1956. We killed most of them when they landed, but he fled with the rest into the mountains. Now, he's gaining popularity with the stupid peasants and must be stopped."

Gomez saluted. They wanted Castro badly. If he could find him, political and monetary reward was assured. He didn't care about the money; it was position and respect he wanted. He'd done well for a poor *campesino* from the country, but *this*…this could mean *really* big things.

"Don't come back until you get him," the general said.

"*Sí, General.* I will succeed." The general returned his salute. Gomez spun and strode out of the headquarters. The general needn't worry. He'd be pursuing this assignment most vigorously. Capturing this bandit would bring recognition and reward that could get Gomez into the highest military and social echelons. Nothing would be allowed to stand in the way of a prompt completion of this mission and his triumphant return to Havana.

"*Capitan*, there's a man coming with a white flag!" Captain Gomez was in his tent looking over the maps on his table when his sergeant burst in. They'd been tracking the rebels for weeks and had yet to see them. Sometimes the locals would say that the rebels had visited their villages recently, but as often as not, their information turned out to be misleading. This Castro seemed to be getting a lot of support from the peasants. The situation was frustrating. Gomez's initial enthusiasm and confidence was beginning to turn to fear that he might not be able to find Castro after all. "He says he wants to talk to you."

The sergeant held open the flap of the tent and Gomez stepped out into the cool morning sun of the mountains. A tall, bearded man with a broad smile walked towards him, guarded by two of Gomez's soldiers. He wore army fatigues and held a white flag on a stick over his head. "*Hola*," said the man. "I've been sent by my *comandante*."

"Have you searched him?" Gomez said to the soldiers.

"*Sí, Capitan*. He's clean."

"Come in then." He motioned the emissary inside his tent. The sergeant and the two soldiers joined them.

"Who are you?" Gomez asked the man when they were seated.

"My name is Camilo," the man said. "*Comandante* Castro has sent me to invite you to come to his camp. He wants to talk to you."

"Why doesn't he come here, himself?"

"Oh, *Capitan*," Camilo laughed. "You know he can't do that. He's the only leader we have. You have many leaders. *Too many leaders*…that's part of the problem. We can't afford to take the chance that *El Comandante* would be captured. He's our only leader."

Gomez motioned to the map. "Where is he?"

"Oh, *Capitan*," Camilo laughed again. "I can't tell you that, but I can take you there."

Gomez thought about this for a moment. It was unlikely that a visit to Castro's camp would present any real danger to him. He hadn't been much of a threat to Castro, so far. There would be no advantage for the rebels to eliminate him. They knew the government would just send someone else out to replace him if he was killed. He did want to meet this Castro. Perhaps by talking with the man he could pick up some clues about how he might be captured. He must be a magnetic figure to have earned the *campesinos'* loyalty and support so completely. He wanted to see what this Castro was all about. When his superiors back in Havana asked him how things were going, he'd at least be able to say something other than, "We've had no luck, yet."

"Okay," Gomez said. "I'll come with you. These men will come, also." He indicated the two soldiers and his sergeant.

"They can't come with you. You must come alone. There's no need for them. You'll be safe with me."

Gomez looked hard at this bearded man with the army fatigues and the broad smile. He seemed surprisingly intelligent. He supposed that he could hold the man as a hostage and try to bargain with Castro for his release…he must be an important man among the rebel group. But bargain for what? Certainly, they wouldn't trade Castro for the emissary. What Gomez wanted was to meet this Castro and that's exactly what was being proposed. "Alright," he said. "I'll come with you."

They'd been walking through the mountain jungle for some time when the bearded rebel turned to Gomez. "I'm sorry, *Capitan*, but I must put this blindfold on you." He held up the same white piece of cloth he'd used on the stick as a flag.

"That's not necessary," Gomez said.

Camilo put up his hand. "I must," he said. He tied the cloth around Gomez's head and made him turn around several times until he was satisfied that Gomez's sense of direction was lost.

With his eyes blindfolded, Gomez tried to gauge direction by the warmth of the sun's rays, but it was midday and directly overhead. Raul took his arm and led him on for another hour. Finally, they stopped, and removed the blindfold. When Gomez opened his eyes, he was staring directly into the intense dark eyes of another tall, bearded man in army fatigues. He looked much like the emissary.

"I'm Fidel Castro," the man said. "Welcome to our camp. You're just in time for lunch. Come and have some chicken…we can't eat it all."

Gomez looked around at the two dozen men who occupied this clearing in the jungle. They eyed him with suspicion. Inside the clearing there was one large tent along with several smaller ones. Chicken for lunch to give me the message that they're doing well and not starving, Gomez thought. He had to admit that they did look well-fed, as well as well-armed.

Castro, Gomez, and Camilo squatted around the campfire. Castro pulled his knife from its sheath and cut a large piece of the chicken that was cooking over the fire. He stabbed it with the point of his knife and offered it over to Gomez. "*Gracias*," Gomez said.

"So," Castro said, "Camilo has been treating you well?"

Gomez looked over at Camilo, who smiled. "He brought me here," Gomez said. "He said you wanted to talk."

Castro cut off a large piece of the chicken for himself. "*Sí*," he said, "I'd like to talk, but first we'll eat this chicken, eh?" Between the three of them, they picked the chicken carcass clean in minutes.

Gomez hadn't realized how hungry he was. The chicken was delicious. He waited until they'd all finished before he took the initiative. These men had been in control of the situation since Camilo had shown up in his camp. He needed to reassert himself and his position. He was, after all, a captain in the army of Cuba.

As difficult and irritating as these men had been to find, they were only lowly rebels. "Thanks for the meal," he said. "Now it's time to talk."

Castro ignored Gomez's statement and wiped his hands on his pants. "How was your chicken?"

Gomez looked at this man…this bearded jungle fighter who claimed to be a revolutionary. He knew some of the man's history. He knew Castro had been born into the family of a wealthy sugar planter. He attended the University of Havana where he'd been a student leader. He even attained a law degree. What was such a man doing here? "The chicken was fine," Gomez said.

Castro stood up. "Let's go to my tent. We'll talk over a glass of *rioja*." Camilo remained behind picking at the chicken carcass. "Sit down," Castro said when they entered the tent. He motioned to a canvas chair next to a small table. He placed two glasses on the table and uncorked a bottle of red wine. He filled both glasses and stood the bottle in the middle of the table. He took a seat across from Gomez and raised his glass. "To Cuba," he said.

Gomez raised his own glass. "To Cuba."

"Why do you hunt me?" Castro said.

"I'm a soldier. You're a bandit," Gomez said.

Castro half rose out of his seat. He leaned across the table and jabbed the air with his finger. "I'm not a bandit! We're revolutionaries! We're going to get rid of that tyrant, Batista, and return our country back to its people! Don't tell me you're not aware of the destitute conditions of Cuba's poor!"

Gomez tried not to reveal the alarm he felt at this sudden impassioned outburst. He hadn't entertained the idea before, but was it possible that Castro was a madman? He picked up his glass and sipped his wine. He returned Castro's glare with passivity. "I apologize, *señor*," he said. "It wasn't my intention to insult you."

Castro relaxed and sank back into his chair. "Would you like a cigar?"

"*Sí, por favor*. A cigar would go very well with the wine."

Castro drew two cigars from the breast pocket of his fatigues and handed one to Gomez. He pulled a cigar cutter from his pocket and snipped the end of his own cigar and then pushed the cutter across the table to Gomez. He struck a stick match on the table and lit Gomez's cigar first and then his own. "More wine?" he said.

Gomez nodded and Castro refilled both of their glasses. "You think you know about me?" Castro said. He leaned his head back and blew smoke toward the top of the tent.

"Some," Gomez said.

"I know some about you, too," Castro said. He smiled at Gomez with raised eyebrows. His face mirrored what he assumed would be Gomez's surprise at this statement.

Gomez *was* surprised but maintained his expression of genial passivity. What could Castro possibly know about him and why would this man care enough to make the effort to find out?

"I know, for instance," Castro said, "that you *are* aware of the deplorable living conditions of the poor, because you used to be one of them."

Castro's eyes penetrated those of Gomez as he spoke. Despite his efforts to remain calm, the intense stare of this man gave Gomez a feeling of discomfort. He shifted in his seat, puffed his cigar, and sipped his wine.

"You escaped your poverty by joining the military. You must be a very clever man to have been able to attend the academy and advance upwards to the rank of captain. Tell me that you remember what living in those poor conditions of your childhood was like."

Gomez nodded. "I remember," he said.

"You must still have family there," Castro said. "Don't you feel badly for them?"

Gomez nodded again. Some distant relatives still lived where he'd grown up. Both his older brother and sister had died when he was still an infant. His mother had died during his own birth and his father had died when Gomez was sixteen. It was then that he left to join the military, but he didn't tell Castro any of this.

"Those are the people we're fighting for," Castro said. "Batista does nothing for them. He acts as though they don't exist, while he and his friends live in luxury. Don't you agree?"

Gomez nodded again. Of course, all Castro said was true, but what did it matter? The *campesinos* had always lived that way.

They would *always* live that way. There was nothing that could be done.

Castro slapped his hand on the table. "Good," he said. "I knew you'd agree. Now, I've brought you here because I want you to help us."

Gomez's eyes widened. Help them? What was he talking about? Gomez was having far too much success with the path he'd chosen to ever consider abandoning it…for any reason, least of all to aid a ragtag group of revolutionaries, who were only going to get themselves killed and him, too, if he did anything to help them.

Castro noted the alarm on Gomez's face. "Don't worry, I don't want you to stop looking for us or following your orders. I only want you to continue to look in the wrong places. And when we attack Havana, I want you and your men to be conveniently elsewhere. We'll certainly be successful. Batista's a coward. Already his hold on the government is weakening. *And* there'll be a very special position in my government for a clever ally, such as yourself." He winked.

Gomez analyzed all that Castro was saying. All he was asking of him was to make himself and his men scarce. No one else had been able to find this man either. "What sort of position?" he said.

"I'm asking you for an important favor," Castro said. "It must, therefore, be an important position. Do we have a bargain?"

Gomez considered the ash at the end of his cigar for a few moments before answering. What did he care whether it was Batista or Castro who prevailed? It was only essential to be on the side of the winner…he could at least afford to wait a while and see how things seemed to be turning out. He looked across the table at Castro. "*Sí*," he said. "We have a bargain, *señor*. My men will not find you."

"*Bueno*!" Castro said, "*bueno*!" He understood this man. Gomez cared nothing for the plight of the poor or for the revolution. He lacked passion for anything but his own advancement. Castro would have preferred it to be otherwise, but now that he knew what motivated Gomez, he could control him. It wouldn't be difficult to find a place for such a man in his government. This Gomez could be useful.

21

Finisterre was moored in a choice location along the pier when *Criollo* entered the harbor of St. Petersburg, Florida. "Looks like she's been here a while," Oliva said. "She's already washed down; sails are furled, and crewmen showered. Let's go in just behind her. The good thing will be that we'll have a solid berth and be able to come and go easily. The bad thing is that we'll have other boats rafting off us. Every crewman from every boat in the raft will have to cross our decks on his way to and from shore. We'll have to sleep with drunks tripping over our winches and lifelines in the dark." He sighed. "Oh well, let's get her cleaned up and get ready for dinner at the yacht club. The rest of the fleet will be in soon."

Wearing their dress whites, the cadets sat at a long table along a wall decorated with pictures of SORC boats and champions of years past. "Send a rum and Coke to that big guy over there with the trophy in front of him," Roberto said to the waiter.

When the drink arrived, Magner looked over to their table, smiled and raised the glass. Roberto raised his in return.

After dinner Magner made his way to the *Criollo's* table and ordered drinks for all who would have one. When the drinks arrived, he offered a toast. "To the brave young cadets from Cuba," he said. "To finish second in such a race is no disgrace. Your courage to race on in such extreme weather conditions, despite having been knocked down, is admirable. Gentlemen, I salute you."

"We put the sails back up because Oliva told us to," José said. "We didn't know there was a choice."

Magner laughed. "Where did you find such brave young men?" he asked Oliva.

Oliva shrugged. "In Cuba."

"Of course," said Magner, "of course. In Cuba. Now, tell me, what about this Castro character? Do you think his revolutionary force stands any real chance of overthrowing Bastista?"

Oliva shrugged again. "I'm not a political person. I know only about boats."

"They have no chance," Carlos said. "Castro's a minor irritation to the government at best. The Cuban military is strong. We have well-trained officers and troops. The revolutionaries are a rag-tag group of misfits, led by a blowhard buffoon."

"It's my understanding he's been running loose in the mountains for years," Magner said. "I've also heard he's stolen large caches of weapons from the federal troops and that his men are now well-armed. They say more peasants join up with him every day."

"We can round him up any time we want to," Carlos said. "Besides, as long as he stays up in the mountains, who cares?"

"What do *you* think?" Magner said to Roberto. "Do you agree with your friend's assessment?"

"Somewhat," Roberto said. "While it's true that Castro seems to be getting more support, it doesn't seem possible that he could actually succeed in overthrowing the government."

"Where's his support coming from?"

"It seems to be coming from a variety of places. He's said to be a charismatic leader who has captured the imagination of many different people. Personally, I must admit that I find him interesting."

Carlos pushed his chair back from the table. "Oh, please!"

"I'm not saying that I agree with his ideas," Roberto said. "I'm just saying that I think I can understand why people are drawn to him."

"Nobody *I know* thinks there's anything good about him!" Carlos said. "I can't believe you're saying these things, Roberto. I'm getting a drink." He left the table and headed for the bar.

"Go on, Roberto. You say he's interesting. What do you mean?"

"Well, here's this guy who already has it made in life. His family owns a sugar plantation. He could have gone into the family business, but instead he gets a law degree and starts taking cases defending the poor. One of his most notable courtroom victories was to get a fair standard of pay for farm workers. So, in the beginning, most of his support was coming from the *campesinos*."

"So, what's different now?"

"Now, there seems to be less negative talk about Castro coming from the upper classes. Everybody knows Batista's government is corrupt. I don't think most people necessarily believe Castro's the leader they want, but in the minds of many, Bastista doesn't represent the best interests of Cuba or its citizens."

Carlos returned, drink in hand. "Hey, *amigos*," he said, "some guys are going to the other side of Tampa, to a place called Ybor City. They say there's a lot of fun to be had over there."

"What you can have over there is a lot of trouble," Magner said. "I'd advise against it."

"You sound like you've had enough anyway," José said.

"I'm going," Carlos said. "You guys can come or not. I don't care."

Roberto awoke to the sound of footsteps coming from the deck above him. It was Carlos, stumbling and cursing his way along the deck until he collapsed in the cockpit. Roberto reached for his watch and leaned toward the light coming through a porthole to read the time. It was almost four o'clock in the morning. He hung the watch back on its hook, rolled over and went back to sleep.

When daylight arrived, Roberto found several of the crew standing over Carlos who was still passed out in the cockpit. "Looks like he really got into it," one of them said.

Roberto knelt over Carlos. His face was a puffy, red mass of welts and bruises. There were scratches on his knuckles and bloodstains on his uniform. "Anybody know what happened?"

No one knew.

"Were any of you out with him last night?"

They all shook their heads.

"Does anybody know who he was with?"

"I think he might have gone with one of the bartenders from the yacht club after they closed up," said a cadet.

"Someone get me a wet cloth. His face is a mess."

Roberto dabbed the cloth on Carlos's broken face. "What happened to you, Carlos? You look like you got hit by a truck."

Carlos moaned.

A police cruiser pulled up next to the dock. Handcuffed in the back of the car was one of the yacht club bartenders. "He doesn't look too good either," said a cadet.

Two policemen got out of the car and approached the boat. One of them prepared to board *Criollo*, but a large, red-headed figure stepped in front of him and blocked his path. "This is a foreign vessel," Magner said. "You must have a permit to board her."

The eyes of the policeman narrowed. "We have reason to believe there's a criminal suspect onboard that boat."

"Perhaps," Magner said, "but you must have a permit to search it. May I have a word with you, officer?"

Magner put his arm around the shoulders of the policeman and led him away from the boat. Roberto saw Magner take out his wallet, flip it open and hand it to the policeman. The policeman studied the wallet for a moment and then looked up at Magner. He shot one more glance at the boat and then motioned to his partner. "Let's go," he said.

Magner walked over to Oliva who had come up on deck. "Get your crew together and set sail back to Cuba as soon as you can," he said. "I've been able to take care of things for now, but whatever has happened sounds serious. Fortunately, I don't think your man was the primary perpetrator. I think he just happened to be in the wrong place at the wrong time."

"Thank you, *señor*," Oliva said. "We'll leave right away."

"No problem," Magner said. "Glad I could help." He walked over to where Roberto and José were standing with the other cadets. "Have a good trip back," he said. "See you next year, I hope."

"Thank you for helping our friend," Roberto said. "Do you know what happened?"

"There was a fight outside a club in Ybor City. Apparently, someone was shot. Your friend wasn't the shooter, but he was there.

Take him home to Cuba and tell him not to go out late at night in strange towns…especially when he's drunk."

"Thank you, Mr. Magner."

"It was nothing. Take care, boys."

22

Havana

December 1958

Alyssa lay with Roberto on the beach at Marianao watching clouds pass across the face of the moon. "It's been a whole year since we first met."

"It's almost 1959," he said. "Time is passing quickly."

"My father wants to see you and José."

"We'd like to see him, too. It's been a while since we've had one of his mojitos."

"No, Roberto, I think it must be something serious. He wouldn't tell me what it's about, but he seems worried."

Roberto looked at her. She was beautiful in any light but laying on her back like this in the moonlight, she was an angel. Her hair fell back away from her face. Her chest rose and fell with her breathing. "What does he need to worry about? He's one of the most powerful men in the country."

"That may be the problem," Alyssa said. "People say Castro's getting stronger every day and it won't be long before he comes charging down out of the mountains and takes over the government. When he does, he's going to kill anyone who's been close to Batista."

"But your father is one of the good ones," Roberto said. "Surely, Castro will understand that. He's done everything he could for the people despite Batista's policies. Everything's going to be okay. When does he want us to come?"

"Can you come tomorrow evening? Whatever it's about, it sounds like he has no time to waste. He said he wants to see the two of you as soon as possible."

"I'll get José and we'll be there," Roberto said. "Your father's a great man. José and I are both prepared to do whatever he believes is necessary."

Alyssa turned toward him. "I love you so much, Roberto. My heart is filled with you." She reached her arms around his neck. "Kiss me, Roberto. Kiss me, now!"

Darkness had fallen when Roberto and José arrived at the Villanueva residence. Alyssa met them at the door. "Ah," she said, "thank God you're here. He's in the library pacing back and forth in front of his desk. I've never seen him like this. I'm scared."

Roberto held her for a moment. "It's alright," he said. "Whatever it is, we'll help him work it out."

The colonel stopped pacing when Roberto and José entered the library. He locked them both in an embrace that seemed to last longer than usual. Roberto raised his eyebrows at Alyssa.

She nodded. See what I mean?

"A *Mojito*, my young friends?" the colonel said.

"Have you ever known me to refuse one of your *Mojitos*, Uncle?" José said.

"Or me?" Roberto said.

"I'll leave you gentlemen to your conversation," Alyssa backed from the room and closed the tall double doors of the library together.

A look passed between Roberto and José. This must *really* be serious. Neither of them could have imagined any conversation occurring between them and Colonel Villanueva, which did not include Alyssa. The colonel prepared the drinks in silence.

He looks tired, thought Roberto.

When the colonel had finished, he handed them each a *Mojito* and raised his own glass. "To Cuba," he said.

"To Cuba." The combination of flavors tasted good. The bite of the rum and the tartness of the lime were softened by the sweetness of the sugar.

The colonel smiled. "The *Mojito*," he said, holding his own glass up to the light. "It's much like life…the sweet and the sour blended with the inflammatory." He moved to where a small table with a lamp stood next to a leather chair. "Put your drinks over here when you're finished," he said. "Then I want the two of you to move the desk."

Roberto and José each took an end of the heavy Castilian desk and moved it from the rug beneath it. Colonel Villanueva drew the carpet away and knelt on the floor. "I'm going to show you something." He slipped a screwdriver beneath the edge of a tile and lifted it up. He lifted another and a rectangular metal plate was revealed. He pried the plate away with the screwdriver.

He stood up and stepped back. "You are the two young men I trust most in the world. My nephew, whom I love like a son, and his best friend, the young man my daughter loves. It's become known to me that Batista plans to flee the country soon. Fidel Castro will then assume power. What that means for me I don't know. Perhaps he'll ask me to assist in the transition of governments. Maybe he'll have me arrested... who knows? If I'm taken from my house, it will certainly be searched, and I have something here that must not be found." He gestured to the hole in the floor. "Take it out."

Inside the hole was a small wooden chest, very old in appearance. They each took an end and lifted it up and onto the tiles. "What's in it?" José said.

The colonel sighed and sank into the leather chair. "Thirteen years ago, a sergeant in the army came to me with this chest in his possession and made me a proposition. He told me that he would be willing to trade it and its contents to me for a recommendation to the military academy. After viewing the contents of the chest, I agreed, and the chest has lain hidden here beneath the floor of my library ever since."

The two cadets sat on the floor next to the chest while the colonel told his story. Roberto's mind began to race. Could it be? Was it possible? Could this be the treasure my father looked for after I stumbled over the pipe on the riverbank?

Roberto shot a glance at Colonel Villanueva. "*Sargento* Gomez gave you this chest?"

"Yes, Roberto," Villanueva said. "Your father was right. There *was* a treasure buried near the Taoro river. Gomez was able to obtain it for himself by deceiving your father and everyone else. Then he brought it to me to trade for an opportunity to be an officer in the army. He trusted me because I knew him from several years earlier when he'd saved Alyssa from drowning at that same beach."

"But why did you hide it? Why did my father never get his reward?"

"I'm sorry, Roberto. This treasure had to remain a secret. I've shared its discovery with no one else until this very night. Not even Juliana or Alyssa know about it. I believe this treasure belongs to the people of Cuba. If any word had gotten out about it, the chest would certainly have been confiscated by the government and evaporated into its halls of corruption, never to be seen again. As long as I was able to maintain my position in the government, I knew Gomez would say nothing. But I don't trust him and now with everything so uncertain, I can't be so sure of his silence. If Castro takes power and gets rid of everyone connected to Batista, as many expect him to, my house may be searched, and the treasure discovered. While Castro professes to be a man of the people, power and riches can corrupt any man. Now, take the lid from the box and see what your father was prevented from finding."

Together, Roberto and José lifted the lid from the chest and lay it on the floor. Speechless, they stared at the sparkling heap of green stones the chest contained.

Villanueva knelt between them. "This chest hasn't been opened since Gomez and I pried the top off when he first brought it to me. I haven't looked at these jewels since. I don't know their value, but they're surely worth many millions."

Roberto and José were mesmerized. "What do you want us to do, Uncle?" José asked.

"You must take the chest away from my house and find a safe hiding place for it. I'm transferring the responsibility for its care to the two of you. You'll know when the time comes to use it and you'll use it wisely."

"But where?" Roberto said. "Where can we hide it so it can't be found?"

"I don't know," Villanueva said, "but wherever it is, don't tell me. I don't want to know. I'm old. I don't know how much torture and interrogation I could endure before I revealed the secret."

"You can count on us, Uncle," José said. "We'll find a safe place for it."

"Yes," Roberto said. "You've done your part. We'll take care of it now."

"What should we do with it?" José said. They were driving away from the Villanueva mansion with a fortune in emeralds in the trunk of the Pontiac.

"There's only one place I can think of, Amigo," Roberto said.

"Where?"

"The *Criollo*."

"The *Criollo*?!"

"*Sí*, we can hide it down in the keel. No one would ever think to look for it there."

"Maybe no one will find it there, but boats can sink."

"*Criollo* is a solid boat. She won't sink. Not while Oliva's on her, anyway. Can you think of any place better, Amigo?"

"No, I can't think of anywhere. How will we get it past Oliva?"

"We won't be able to," Roberto said. "We'll have to take him into our confidence."

"My uncle didn't tell anyone about the treasure for the thirteen years it was in his possession and we're going to tell someone about it on the first night?"

"We have no choice."

"Yes, by all means, hide it here," Oliva said, when they showed him the treasure.

"Are you sure?" Roberto said. "It could be very dangerous. I don't want you to feel like we're taking unfair advantage of you."

"Even God must wonder where time began and to what purpose he's being used," Oliva said. "The *Criollo* will be proud to be the repository for this hope of the Cuban people."

23

January 1959

The doors were locked. That was odd. Alyssa turned and walked back down the steps. This morning was the beginning of second-semester classes. Why would the doors be locked? A car full of students came honking down the street. Cuban flags fluttered from the car's windows.

"Alyssa, get in! Come with us! Batista has fled the country! Castro's coming!"

They hadn't gone far before traffic began to back up. Cars were parked on the sidewalks and in the middle of the streets. "I can't go any further," the driver said. "We'll have to get out here and walk."

When they reached Plaza Central, the sidewalks were lined with people cheering and waving flags. More people and flags were hanging out of open windows in the floors above. The country had gone crazy. They were finally free of the dictator. Everyone was excited about Castro. It looked like all of Cuba had fallen at his feet.

Alyssa hung back from the curb where everyone was pressing forward to get a better view. I guess I'm happy Batista's gone, she thought, but what will happen to Papi? These people are too excited. They look like sheep, bleating and jostling each other. They don't know where they're being led — to greener pastures or to the slaughterhouse? Batista was bad, but how much do we really know about this Castro? Time will tell. Let him prove himself.

A cheer arose from the crowd. It was hard to see from her place against the wall, but then there he was in his beard and army fatigues. Sitting up high on one of the big army tanks rumbling into Havana was Fidel Castro. He looked almost shy and overwhelmed by his reception. Then Alyssa gasped and shrank back against the wall. "Oh, my God!" she said aloud. Sitting next to Castro atop the tank, smiling and waving, was Diego Montalvo.

Alyssa returned home after watching Castro's entrance into Havana. She went into the library when she heard her father talking with her grandfather, Isaak.

"Batista's gone," she said.

"We know," Villanueva said. "Your grandparents are leaving the country."

"What?"

"I've seen this story unfold before," Isaak said. "Your grandmother and I watched as Hitler's power grew until we were lucky to escape. Mussolini, Franco, Stalin...all narcissistic sociopaths...a disorder of the mind that's the enemy of good. They're mad for power and must win every challenge, no matter the cost, even if it's against their own people. This man is no different. It can happen anywhere a naive populace is blind to the reality of a charismatic politician. We're leaving for New York before the firing squads begin. Juliana's at our house helping your grandmother pack."

"Oh, *mi abuelo*. Not, again!"

"I'm afraid so, my dear. I've been trying to convince your father to leave with us, but without success."

They made tearful good-byes and Isaak returned home to do his own packing. Alyssa collapsed in a chair near her father's desk. "Why do you keep working, *Papi,* when Bastista has left the country?"

"I don't work for the leader of Cuba," Alyssa. "I work for the people of Cuba. And they're still here."

"I just saw Fidel Castro come into the city," Alyssa said. "He was riding on top of an army tank. The people are going crazy."

Her father nodded. "I'm not surprised."

"What will you do, Papi? Will you go to see him?"

"They know where I live," he said. "They'll find me soon enough."

"Diego Montalvo was sitting next to Castro on the tank."

"Really?" the colonel said. "The young man you dated before you met Roberto?"

"*Sí*, Papi."

Alyssa recalled Diego's words on the day they'd parted, and a chill ran through her. "Things are changing in Cuba," he'd said. "You may soon find yourself very sorry that you did this to me."

24

A soldier in army fatigues holding a rifle stepped in front of him. "Who are you?"

"Who are *you*," Roberto said, "and why are you standing in front of this house?"

"We have orders to turn away anyone who tries to enter."

"What's the matter with you," Roberto said. "Can't you see I'm in a military uniform, too?"

"Yes, I can see that," said the soldier. "But you still haven't told me why you're here."

"I'm Roberto Valiente. I'm a friend of the Villanueva family. Why are *you* here?"

"We've come to arrest Colonel Villanueva. He's gathering his papers before we take him in."

"Let me pass," Roberto said. "I may be able to help."

The two soldiers looked at one other and stepped aside. Roberto entered the house and adjusted his eyes to the dimness of the living room. Alyssa and Juliana were on the living room sofa. Juliana rocked back and forth, crying, and talking, but her speech was unintelligible. Alyssa was holding and comforting her. She looked up when Roberto came into the room. Tears streamed from her own eyes. "Oh, Roberto, they've come to take my father. My mother's distraught."

Roberto went to the sofa and put his arms around them both. "There, there," he said. "I'm here now." Alyssa lay her head on his chest and let her emotions out in loud sobs.

Behind her, a tall man in a gray business suit came into the room from the library. When the tall man saw Roberto, his face reddened in rage. "I gave orders that no one would be allowed to enter this house! Who is this man? Who let him in here?"

Alyssa brushed the tears from her face and stood to face the tall man. "This is Roberto Valiente, the man I left you for, you bastard! He's a man, not a marionette!" She turned back to Roberto. "And this rude errand boy of our great new leader is Diego Montalvo. He's come to take my father to jail."

Roberto crossed the floor and extended his hand. "Diego," he said, "how can I be of assistance?"

Diego took a step backward. "Roberto Valiente," he said. "It's been a long time."

"Yes, it has," Roberto said. "It's been a long time since we were boys playing games."

Diego acknowledged Juliana and Alyssa holding each other on the sofa. "I know this must look bad to you," Roberto," he said, "but it's necessary. This is happening all over Cuba. All those who were in governmental positions under Batista must be rounded up. Each case will be looked at individually to determine if any crimes have been committed against the people of Cuba. If none are found against Alyssa's father, he'll be released."

"I'm confident you will find no crimes committed against the people by Colonel Villanueva," Roberto said, "but I'd like to have a moment alone with him before you take him."

Diego considered this request for a moment. He was taking the Colonel to jail. Except for the emotional scenes of the women, things were going smoothly. Roberto was showing him respect for his authority. Why not allow him some time with the old man? That would allow him to have some time with Alyssa. He stood aside from the library entrance. "Go ahead," he said.

Roberto stepped past Diego. He gave a wink to Alyssa as he closed the door behind him. The colonel stood at his desk with his back straight, but weariness was in his face. He looked up when Roberto entered and nodded. "Hello, Roberto," he said. "They've come to arrest me for treason."

"Treason! Diego didn't tell me that."

"It's alright," the colonel said. "I've been expecting it. I think I have enough people who will come forward and speak for me to avoid a guilty verdict."

"I'm sure you do," Roberto said. "Is there anything I can do for you?"

"Thank you, Roberto. Please take care of Juliana and Alyssa while I'm away. Juliana's taking things very hard."

"I will," Roberto said.

"I knew I could count on you, Roberto. Did you and José find someplace to hide the chest?"

"Yes. We put it...."

"Don't tell me. That way I can honestly answer in total ignorance if anyone brings it up."

"I thought no one else knew about it," Roberto said.

"Only that weasel, Gomez. He was a soldier in Batista's army, but I wouldn't be surprised if he figures out a way to profit from all of this. If he finds out that I've been arrested, he may try to make things better for himself and improve his position with Castro by betraying our little secret. Whatever happens to me, you must promise to never give up the treasure."

"I promise," Robert said.

"*Bueno.*"

Roberto's wink before he disappeared behind the library door lifted Alyssa. She turned on Diego. "How can you do this to my family? You come in here all flush with your newfound good fortune, throwing your weight around. You're nothing more than a paid goon!"

"Roberto's father rolls cigars in my father's factory, Alyssa...a common laborer! What are you thinking, Alyssa? You should never have left me for him. I tried to tell you things were going to be different."

"I knew it! You're doing this to my father just to get back at me, aren't you? You're a sad little worm, Diego. You think you can impress me with your connection to Castro, your position, and your power? Well, you can't. You want me to fall on my knees and tug at your pant leg, asking for forgiveness for my father? I won't. I won't because he's innocent. He's done nothing but fight for the people of Cuba all his life. And now you've come here to drag him away to jail like a common criminal. You want me to be impressed, Diego Montalvo? All right, I'm impressed. I'm impressed with what an ass you've managed to make of yourself!"

Diego broke his eyes from the heat of Alyssa's glare. Her mother continued to cry into her handkerchief, rocking forward and back. "I don't like seeing your mother cry any more than you do," he said. "But I have no choice in what is happening here today. Believe me, Alyssa, better it is me than someone else. I'll see to it that your father has a fair trial."

"I'm so sure," Alyssa said.

"I have influence in the new government," Diego said. "I give you my word that I'll do everything in my power to help your father."

Alyssa suppressed an impulse to continue her sarcasm. Was he being genuine? Maybe he would be able to intervene for her father, as he was promising. If he was as important as he was making out, perhaps he really could exert some positive influence on the outcome of the case. She relented. "All right, Diego, I'll take you at your word and wait to see what you can do."

25

"Do you have any money?" José asked.

"Only what I was able to sew into the linings and hems of our dresses," Alyssa said. "They confiscated my father's bank account and all his assets. And now they're evicting us from our own house. We're being left with nothing. Thank God you came to get us."

"How's your mother?" Roberto asked.

"When the court announced my father's sentence, she broke down completely. Sometimes she seems to think she's back in Poland. I don't think she even knows who she is any more."

"The bastards," José said.

"The trials lasted for weeks," Alyssa said. "It was horrible. Many were executed. Despite the testimony of many supporters, my father was given a sentence of life imprisonment. They really wanted to kill him because he was so high up in Batista's government. It was only the stories of witness after witness of how he had helped them that managed to save his life.

"I got Mami home, but her mind was gone. Yesterday, the soldiers came again. They were drunk and they smelled bad. They ransacked everything, took whatever they wanted and broke the rest. They told us we had twenty-four hours to leave our house, because it had been confiscated by the state. That's when I called you."

"The bastards," José said again. "I'll take you to my father's house. You can stay there."

"Maybe it's better for you to stay with my parents," Roberto said. "My mother can help you with Juliana."

Alyssa shook her head and sighed. "Whatever the two of you decide. My mind is too numb to think. Everything's happened so fast. We don't want to be a burden to anyone."

"Nonsense," Roberto said. "My parents will insist upon it."

Ernesto, Violetta, and Maria were at the Valiente house when they arrived. *"Dios mio,"* Violetta said to Ernesto when she saw the condition of Juliana and heard the story of Colonel Villanueva's imprisonment. "My God, what's happening to our country?"

"I can't believe it," Ernesto said.

"I always imagined Alyssa's mother to be a person of style and beauty, but this poor woman looks like she's been living in the streets," Maria said.

Roberto gathered them together. "They've had a rough time of it. Juliana's not the woman she used to be. It's been too much for her and she's withdrawn from the world. Castro's ruined a lot of lives."

"I thought things would be better when Castro took over," Ernesto said, "but things are not turning out as I'd hoped."

Violetta and Maria went out to the car to help Alyssa. "Can this really be happening?" Violetta said. "Can this really be your mother?

"Yes, it is so," Alyssa said. "They've put my father in Matanzas prison for the rest of his life and turned my mother into what you see here."

"I'm so sorry," Violetta said. "This is all so horrible."

"It is horrible and it's unfair," Alyssa said. "But I swear to you on my life, Violetta, that this is not over. It's not right for them to treat good people like my parents this way. Someday, they're going to pay for what they've done. I'm not finished with them, Violetta. Our future might be uncertain, but I am not. I'll do whatever it takes to right the wrongs that've been done to my family."

The men went outside while the women put Juliana to bed. They leaned their backs against the car, smoked cigars and talked. "Is it alright if they stay here with you for a while, Papi?" Roberto said.

"*Sí*, of course. But what will *you* do, Machito?"

"I don't know. I don't think I can stay at the Naval Academy any longer. They've hastened our training, so that we'll graduate before the end of the year, but I can't imagine serving a government as cruel as this one has become."

"Then I'm going to quit, too," José said. "It's been my dream for a long time to be a naval officer, but I guess a lot of dreams have been lost around here, lately."

"Are you sure, Amigo?"

"I'm sure. I don't want to stay if you're not there, Roberto. And I can't support what's happening to Cuba, either."

"They'll arrest you both," Ernesto said.

Roberto pushed himself away from the car and turned to face his father. "I know, Papi," he said. "I've been thinking about that. I was going to ask you if I could use your boat."

"My boat?"

"I was thinking we could take it to the United States."

"You would take the *Mojito*? To the U.S.?" Ernesto looked across the water to the land he'd always imagined to be somewhere out there, beyond the horizon. "Not without me," he said. "If you're going, then I'm going with you."

"What?" Roberto said. "I never thought you'd be willing to leave Cuba."

Ernesto spat on the ground. "Castro has nationalized the cigar factory. Damn *communistas*. Already, I can see it becoming a bureaucratic nightmare."

"What about Mami?"

"She'll come with us. The communists have closed our church. They don't believe in religion, so they don't want anybody else to either. We've gone to church all our lives. Without a place to worship God, we're lost. Besides, who wants to live in a country that keeps its people from leaving? There is something wrong with such a country."

"And Tomo?"

"He can come, too."

"And Maria?"

"Her husband is a devoted backer of Castro. I think she'll want to stay with him."

"How many people can your boat hold?" José said.

"I think eight with no problem," Ernesto said. "Maybe ten."

"Then my father and I would like to go, too. He's always wanted to go the United States. There's nothing here for him that he can't find there."

"With Alyssa and Juliana, that would make seven," Roberto said. "What do you think, Papi?"

Ernesto rubbed his chin. Then he looked out across the water again. "I think, yes," he said. "I believe we can do it. It's only ninety miles to Key West. But we must go soon. Already it's hard to get gasoline."

"*Muchas gracias, señor* Valiente," José said. "Thank you for letting us go with you."

"*De nada*," Ernesto said. "It's nothing. I was hoping that you'd come with us and bring your father. We may need help with the engine." He feigned a couple of jabs to José's stomach and went in the house to see how the women were doing with Juliana.

"What're we going to do about the treasure?" José said after Ernesto left.

"I don't know," Roberto said. "I hate to leave without it, but I'm afraid to take it on my father's boat. What if the damn thing sinks or we get boarded by a patrol boat? If we see an opportunity to use it to help our people, we can always come back. I don't think getting back into the country would be all that difficult. It's getting out that's the hard part."

That evening, Roberto sat with Alyssa on the beach near the house. He told her about their escape plan. "We're going to pretend that we're going out fishing. When we're out of sight of land, we'll turn and head north for Florida. Before they figure out that we're not coming back, it'll be dark, and we'll be in international waters."

Alyssa looked out to sea for long moments and then began to cry. "You're very brave, Roberto," she managed through her tears. "I know you have to go, but I also know that I can't go with you."

"I won't go without you."

"You *must* go, Roberto. You'll surely be arrested and put in jail like my father if you stay, or maybe even be shot. But you know I can't leave my parents."

Roberto took her in his arms. "What choice do we have? And your mother can come."

"But I can't leave my father. I have to stay and do whatever I can to get him out of that terrible prison."

"What can you do that hasn't already been tried?"

"You're probably right, I may not be able to do anything. But everything's happening so fast, my head is spinning. I need time to think. Please?"

"I won't leave without you,"

"You have to leave, Roberto. Like you just said, you have no choice. I'll not see both of the men I love most in the world behind the bars of Castro's jails, or worse. And José must go, too."

Ernesto shared the plan to leave the country with Violetta and Maria. "I can't go," Maria said. "My husband thinks Castro is the best thing that's ever happened to Cuba. I could never get him to leave."

"Then I can't go either," Violetta said. "I hate what's happening in our country, but I can't leave Maria."

"Go, Mami," Maria said. "I'll be fine."

"We must go," Ernesto said.   "And it must be tomorrow…there's no time to waste. Maria's husband is a Fidelista. She's made her choice and wants to stay with him."

Violetta began to cry. "It's so hard, Ernesto. It's not so easy for me."

"I'm so sorry, Maria," Ernesto said. Tears rolled down his face. "We have to go. This is our only chance." Violetta was sobbing, too. Her hands flitted about in her lap like birds with no place to rest.

Maria put her arms around her. "No, Mami," she said. "Don't cry. I'm happy for you. It's the right thing for you to do. If it weren't for my husband, I'd bring the children and come, too."

Violetta clasped her arms tight around Maria, whose words of encouragement had only seemed to make her cry harder. When it came time for Maria to return home, Violetta wouldn't release her.

Maria tried to pry herself loose. "I have to go, Mami," she said. "My husband will get suspicious about where I've been, and he'll want to know the reason." Ernesto and Roberto helped free her from Violetta's grip.

Ernesto brushed the tears from his eyes. "We'll be ready for you when your husband comes to his senses and realizes the mistake he's making supporting Castro. Someday, we'll be together again in America. I know it."

After Maria left, Roberto walked back down to the beach with Alyssa. "One woman alone against Castro is a hopeless crusade," he said. "You have no money, and you no longer have any influence in this country, Alyssa. This is not the same Cuba that used to fall on its knees in front of you and grant your every wish."

"Please, Roberto," she said. "My mother's a shattered mess and my father's been sentenced to life in prison. I think I know which Cuba I'm living in."

"I'm sorry, but you'll only end up wasting your own life trying to get him out. I know he'd want you to come with us. Maybe we can do something for him from the U.S."

Alyssa sighed. "Alright, Roberto, maybe you're right. I'll go ask my father what he thinks we should do. José can take Mami and me to the prison early tomorrow morning before he comes to take you to the dock. I'll ask my father if we should go or stay. If he says we should go, then we'll kiss him good-bye and meet the rest of you at the boat."

"Okay," Roberto said. "Get your father's approval. He knows there's no future for you here. I'm sure he'll say, yes."

26

"We'll meet you at the boat in two hours," José said when he dropped Alyssa and Juliana outside the prison gates. "You must be there. We'll look suspicious enough as it is, going out fishing so late in the morning. If you decide you need to stay in Cuba, we'll understand. My father said to tell you that he'll leave the keys in his car at the marina. He wants you to have it if it turns out that you stay here."

"I understand, Amigo. If Papi says it's okay for us to go, we'll be there. If you don't see us, it's because he needs us here in Cuba. And if we must stay, please thank Uncle Enrique for the generosity of his car."

A guard with a flashlight led them up a flight of stairs and down a dim hallway on the second floor of the prison. The conditions made Alyssa feel sick. She pressed a sleeve to her nose to block the foul odors, but she couldn't keep from hearing the cries of despair coming from every direction. The floor was wet from leaking pipes. As they walked, she stared at the guard's back to avoid seeing anything that might be crawling in the hallway.

"Oh, Papi," she said when they reached her father's cell. My god, she thought, he looks so pale. He's aged years in only a few weeks.

"Alyssa. Juliana. It's so good to see you both. Mami is no better?"

"I'm afraid not, Papi. She eats. She sleeps. She'll go where I lead her without complaint, but she's not the woman she once was. All this craziness has been too much for her."

"I'm sorry, Alyssa. Your mother and I have lived our lives. To have all this adversity at the end is unhappy, but we've had our share of good years. You're young. You can still make a life for yourself."

"They've taken our house, Papi. We're living with Roberto's family. I didn't want to tell you, but I knew you'd want to know."

"Our house? *Dios mio.* I knew they'd search it after I was arrested, but to confiscate our home. No, that's just too terrible. I'm so sorry, my child. I'm helpless to do anything."

Alyssa moved closer to the cell and began to whisper. "Papi, Roberto has a plan." She looked at her watch. "He wants Mami and me to meet him and his family and José and Uncle Enrique at his father's boat in one hour. We're to pretend that we're going out fishing, but we'll really be going to the U.S."

Villanueva said nothing, but only looked at Alyssa and then at his wife.

"What do you think, Papi? Should we go?"

"*Sí*, of course I think you should go, my daughter. I hesitate only because I realize I'm looking at you both for the last time."

"Oh, Papi, I don't want to leave you alone."

"Ssshhh, my child. I'll be fine," he said. "There's nothing you can do for me here. In everyone's life there must always be a final good-bye. I want you to go and to take your mother with you. It will make me happy to know that you're both safe in America with Roberto and José."

"Oh, Papi, Papi, Papi. I love you so much. This is all so wrong for you to be locked up in here."

"Wipe your tears and don't worry about me, Alyssa. I'll ask them to bring me books. Finally, I'll be able to catch up on my reading. Now, kiss me quickly and go. There isn't much time left for you to get to the boat. You must hurry." He kissed and hugged them through the bars of the cell. "I love you, Alyssa. I love you, Juliana. Good-bye. Now go." When the metal door at the end of the hallway slammed shut and he knew they were gone, Colonel Villanueva sank to his knees and wept uncontrollably.

They'd nearly reached the bottom of the stairs, when Alyssa saw a tall, familiar figure approaching and her heart stopped.

"Hello Alyssa," Diego said. "I'm so happy to see you. I was told you were here. My office is just across the street, so I thought I'd come over and have a little chat."

Oh, my god, she thought, not Diego of all people. She tried to squeeze past him. "I have nothing to say to you, Diego," she said.

Diego grabbed her arm. "But you must talk to me," he said. "This is official business."

"Let go of me, you pig!" She tried to pull herself free from his grasp. "Your words mean nothing to me."

"On the contrary, you will soon come to realize that my words are all you have, Alyssa." He called to two men standing near the building entrance. "Guards! Bring these two women to the interrogation room." He turned and walked ahead of them down the hall. His shoes made authoritative staccato sounds against the old wooden floors and echoed off the concrete walls.

Alyssa sagged. Her body felt tired and heavy. She felt the guards gripping her arms and she moved along with them. Her legs moved only because they were half carrying her. The guards were strong, their force was uncompromising. She hadn't the strength to resist. They sat her in the interrogation room. She slumped forward and buried her head in her hands. Moments ago, there was precious hope, now devastating despair settled over her.

Diego sat across the table from her. "Why are you making such a fuss, Alyssa? I only want to talk to you."

"Please leave us alone," she said. "Haven't you done enough to ruin our lives?"

"I only want to make certain that you're alright, Alyssa. I want to assure myself that you're being sufficiently cared for."

"We're fine. We don't need your concern, Diego."

"Where are you living?"

"If you must know, we're living with Roberto's family. It's none of your business, Diego, but they were kind enough to take us in after *you* took our home from us."

"You're living in that hovel? I won't allow it…it's beneath your dignity, Alyssa. Here is my proposal. How would you like to live in a modest, but very nice guesthouse on my family's estate here in Havana? You'll live in a manner to which you are more accustomed. I'll check in on you now and then to make sure you're doing all right and have everything you need."

"We don't need your charity, Diego," Alyssa said. "We're fine where we are. Just…leave…us…alone."

"Nonsense," Diego said. "You're not understanding me, Alyssa. I am insisting."

Alyssa stared across the table at Diego. Oh God, oh God, I just want to take my fists and smash in that stupid grinning face of his. This arrogant bastard is holding our fate in his hands and I'm helpless to do anything about it. Roberto, my dearest Roberto, I'm trapped. I love you so much. The only thing I want is to be with you, but there's nothing I can do. Nothing.

27

José laid a hand on Roberto's shoulder. "Come, my friend, it's no use waiting any longer. Pacing up and down the dock is not helping. If we don't go now, we could all be in trouble. Alyssa loves her father very much. She must have decided she needed to stay here and do whatever she can for him."

"You go ahead. I'm going to stay and help Alyssa."

"You'll be no help to her. You can't stay, you'll be shot for desertion. Once we get everyone safely up to Floride, we'll see what we can do from there."

Roberto nodded. "Okay, I know you're right, Amigo. I didn't want to stop hoping, but we've waited long enough. Let's go."

Roberto and José cast off the dock lines and Ernesto started the engine. They motored out of the harbor, past El Morro and on out into the Gulf Stream. Enrique watched his red Pontiac get smaller and smaller.

The dock master watched them leave. It seemed foolish to go out fishing this late in the morning. He was to inform the authorities if anyone looked like they were trying to escape from Cuba, but he'd known Ernesto Valiente for years and wasn't suspicious. He also knew that the two young men on the boat were cadets at the Naval Academy. His only concern was that they wouldn't catch many fish, due to their late start.

"We'll cruise along with the Gulf Stream until we're out of sight of land," Ernesto said. "When we no longer see any other boats, we'll turn up and head north for Florida." He surveyed the sky. The weather was pleasant enough. The breeze was light and there were no waves, only smooth ocean swells which the boat rode without difficulty.

Everyone was quiet, thinking of those they had left back on the island. Tomo sat on the motor box and watched the wake. Ernesto watched the compass and scanned the horizon for patrol boats. Enrique listened to the engine.

José and Roberto went below to get some sleep. A long night was ahead of them. They lay on their bunks and stared at the cabin ceiling. "She's a strong woman," José said. "She'll be alright. After we get settled in the U.S., we'll come back for her."

"Yes," Roberto said.

"We can come back and get Alyssa and the treasure."

"*Sí*," Roberto said. "When we come back, we'll get the treasure, too."

Violetta sat near Tomo on the side of the engine box and looked off toward Cuba. "Our island is so beautiful," she said to no one in particular. "I miss Maria so much. Do we really have to leave?" No one answered.

Ernesto slapped the compass – first lightly and then two hard ones. "Dammit," he said.

"What is it?" Enrique said.

"Damn compass. It keeps getting stuck." Ernesto slapped the compass several more times.

"Can you navigate without it?"

"We can use Cuba as a landmark, while we can still see it. But that won't be for much longer. We can tell East and West from the path of the sun. When the sun goes down, we'll be turning up toward Florida and can use the stars to tell us which way is North. It won't be exact, but the United States is a big country. It would be hard to miss it."

Cuba was first to disappear over the horizon. It was followed not long afterward by the sun. Enrique, Violetta and Tomo watched as the orange ball first touched the horizon of water and then began to melt into it. "It looks so big," Violetta said.

"Yes, and see how fast it sinks," Enrique said.

"That's always been interesting to me," Ernesto said from the wheel. He took a last bearing on the westerly direction to gauge which way was North. "When you're out at sea, you can watch the journey of the sun from start to finish. It takes all day for it to move across the sky and then, in a matter of only a few seconds, it slips over the edge of the earth and is gone." He spun the wheel to the left and the boat turned. Then he turned the wheel back to its neutral position. "There," he said. "I think we're headed north."

He watched with the others the place where the sun had gone down. The sky was going through stages of red and orange and reflected off the clouds and the water. "Red sky at night, sailors' delight," he said.

"The weather will be good tomorrow?" Enrique said.

"That's what they say, but they say a lot of things and they're not always right. It's a generality." The sky continued to darken into night and Ernesto began to search the Eastern sky.

"What are you looking for?" Enrique said.

"I'm trying to find the evening stars. They rise in the East, but there's low cloud cover over there and I can't see them." He looked to the sky in front of them. "Maybe I can find the North Star."

"Any luck," Enrique asked after a few minutes.

"No," Ernesto said. "There're too many clouds ahead of us, too." He slapped the compass again, but again failed to evoke a response. "Damn!" He knocked on the side of the companionway. "Roberto! José! Come up here. I need your help."

Roberto and José scrambled up to the cockpit. "What is it?"

"The damn compass quit working and I can't find the North Star. Can you see it?"

Roberto and José each took their own turns slapping the compass, which remained stuck on 87 degrees, nearly due east.

"Where's the Big Dipper?" Roberto said. "If we can find the Big Dipper, we can follow the line of the two end stars up to the Little Dipper. The North Star is the brightest star in the Little Dipper."

"I think I see it!" José said. "Look! There!" He pointed a little to the left of the direction Ernesto was steering. "See, to the left of that cloud is the handle. Then the cloud and then, on the right, the last two stars of the bucket."

"Yes," Roberto said. "I see it. I think you have it. Steer a little more to port, Papi. More, more, there, that's it. What do you think, Amigo?"

"I think that's about right," José said. "The Little Dipper and the North Star are hidden by the clouds but lining up the two end stars of the Big Dipper is a good idea. I think our heading now is just about parallel to them."

Two hours later, they were still unable to see the Little Dipper or the North Star. Ernesto attempted to stay on course by keeping the boat in a steady orientation to the direction of the waves, which had kicked up with an evening breeze. Now and then, Roberto and José were able to see a portion of the Big Dipper through the clouds and give him approximate navigational corrections. Violetta and Tomo sat together on the back of the engine box. Tomo followed the phosphorescent trails of water left by the boat's wake. When the light emanating from Cuba disappeared over the horizon Violetta began to emit wails of agony. While she'd been able to see a remnant of the island, she was able to tolerate the pain of leaving. When it vanished, unbearable sorrow overcame her. Suddenly, her wails terminated with a single piercing scream of "M-a-r-i-a!"

"No," Tomo said. "Don't!"

The men looked back from their navigating. Violetta had climbed onto the stern of the boat. Before they could reach her, she jumped off, feet-first, into the churning water behind them and disappeared beneath the surface. Her feet and legs were working, as though she were trying to run back to her home and her daughter. Ernesto cut the throttle, but they were still coasting away from where Violetta had leaped into the water. He had kept the running lights off, as a precaution against detection by patrol boats, but now he flicked the switch for the stern light. The light's purpose was to alert other boats to their position, not to illuminate, but it was better than nothing in the darkness of the open ocean.

Roberto jumped over the stern and swam to where she'd disappeared. José was close behind him. Ernesto spun the wheel and turned the boat around. He followed the phosphorescent splashing of Roberto and José and then cut the engine, so they could hear. They called from all sides of the boat. Roberto and José dove, returned to the surface, and dove again until they were exhausted. Finally, they could do no more and were helped back aboard the boat in disbelief of what had just happened. The group stood in silence and peered out into the darkness. Violetta had been there, moaning her distress, and then she was gone with no more trace than a stone.

Ernesto supported himself at the stern, his hands gripping the gunwale, then began to collapse, sliding down to his knees until only his head and arms rested on the back of the boat. He stared down at the black water. After a time, he rolled to one side and sat on the floor with his back against the boat and looked from face to face. "I should never have made her leave Maria. It wasn't fair. I should have listened to her." He put his head in his hands. "I should have put a life jacket on her, as soon as it got dark." Tears streamed down his face. "Violetta…my poor little Violetta. What have I done?"

Roberto sat next to him and put an arm around his shoulders. "There was nothing we could do, Papi," he said through his own tears. "Castro took her heart, but God has her soul."

The men took turns kneeling next to Ernesto and offering words of solace. They said a prayer for the soul of Violetta. Then they sat with their backs against the sides of the cockpit and stared into the darkness. Each man searched his brain for something else that could be done, but there was nothing.

An hour passed before José lifted himself and went to the wheel. He turned the key and pushed the start button. The engine turned over but didn't start. He pushed the button again, and again it failed to catch. Roberto rose to help him, but the motor refused to start. "Papi," he said. "Would you try it, please? We can't stay here like this. We must get moving."

Ernesto stared toward the sound of his name without comprehension.

Roberto shook his shoulder. "Papi," he said. "We have to get going. Please, Papi."

Ernesto looked to where José was standing at the wheel. Their situation came back to him. He wiped the tears from his eyes with the sleeves of his shirt and rose to his feet. With Roberto's assistance, he made his way forward to the steering station, where he went through the same process as José and Roberto, achieving the same result…nothing. He tried several more times.

Enrique motioned for Tomo to move, raised the engine box and examined the motor in the weak illumination provided by the stern light. He watched and listened, as Ernesto continued to turn the engine over. He reached down and disconnected the line that led from the fuel tank to the fuel pump. He felt the end of the line. It was dry. "Ernesto, my friend," he said. "Even I cannot fix this problem…we're out of gas."

The crew looked to their captain. "It was all I could get," Ernesto said. "I thought it would be enough. I thought we would be there by now."

"I wish we knew where the hell we are," Roberto said.

"We have the sail," José said. "It's not much, but let's raise it. Maybe we'll be able to see land when the sun comes up."

When morning arrived, they didn't see any land. All they could see was water… lots of water, spreading out in all directions.

José nodded at the rising sun. "At least we know which direction is east."

"The question is, which way is Florida?" Roberto said.

"I think we should keep going north," Ernesto said. "The U.S. has got to be up there somewhere."

Roberto noted the deep blue river of water they'd traveled in the day before was no longer visible. "We've lost the Gulf Stream," he said.

When midday arrived, they still could see no land. José stood up and pointed. "What's that? It looks like a ship."

"It *is* a ship, and it looks like it's coming in our direction!" Roberto said.

"Yes," Ernesto said, "it does. I just hope it's not Cuban."

They watched as the ship approached, gradually growing larger. Finally, they were able to see a red, white and blue flag, waving in the noonday sun. "It's British!" Roberto shouted. They took off their shirts and began to wave them.

"I think it's slowing down," José said.

"Yes," Roberto said. "It's slowing and it's turning our way!"

The cargo ship towered over them. The ship's captain, dressed in a blue uniform with gold braid on his cap, came to the rail and looked down at them. "Where are you going?" he called.

The older men understood only Spanish, but both Roberto and José understood English. "The United States!" Roberto yelled up to him. "Florida! We've just escaped from Cuba!"

"Then, you're going the wrong way," the captain said. "If you keep going in your current direction, you'll end up in the middle of the Atlantic Ocean. Take your sail down. We'll radio the United States Coast Guard. They'll come and get you."

The captain left the rail for a few minutes but returned with a canvas bag tied to a line. He lowered the bag into the cockpit of the *Mojito*. Inside were two loaves of bread, some fruit, and a bottle of scotch.

"Thank you, sir," Roberto said. "Your generosity is appreciated more than you can know."

The captain smiled and tipped his cap. "Good luck, gentlemen. *Vaya con Dios!*"

The ship's diesels powered up again and it steamed away. The men of the *Mojito* sat on the floor of the cockpit and leaned against the sides of the boat. They divided up the bread and fruit. Then they opened the bottle of scotch and passed it from one to another and waited for the Coast Guard.

28

"How convenient," Alyssa, murmured to her mother when they were shown into the guesthouse Diego had promised them...the house was on the same property as the Montalvo family compound where Diego lived with his parents. "It *is* quite a nice house and it's far enough from the main house to appear correct and proper, but close enough to allow him easy access. I wonder when the first knock will come...in the middle of the night...some pleasant afternoon when he decides to just 'happen by?' Oh, Mami, what have we gotten ourselves into?"

But no knocks came. Each morning fresh groceries and flowers appeared outside the front door of the guesthouse. Diego was being a perfect gentleman.

"I suppose we could try to escape, Mami," Alyssa said, as she brushed her mother's hair. "It seems like we can come and go as we please. But where could we go that they wouldn't find us? I know things could be worse. You still don't talk to me, Papi's in prison and Roberto and José have gone to the U.S., but we're all still alive. Many have not been so lucky. I guess we have everything we need. We'll just stay here until we're strong enough to decide what to do. After all that's happened, I'm too tired to think clearly. When we've had time to rest and adjust to all this upheaval, maybe then we can do something."

It was weeks before Alyssa awoke with the resolve that it was time for them to venture out of doors. "Look at us, Mami. We're both turning pale from being inside so long. Nothing's going to change. We just have to accept that this is our life, now, and start living it, because it's the only one we have. I'm talking to you like you know what I'm saying. I don't even know if you can hear me. For you to escape Hitler only to become an innocent victim of this madman is just too awful."

She dressed herself and Juliana. "Okay, let's go for a walk, Mami. We need fresh air." Juliana walked slowly with Alyssa's support. They had managed two sides of the block and were turning the corner to walk down side number three when Alyssa saw Diego striding toward them, wearing a broad smile.

"It gives me much pleasure to see the two of you out enjoying this splendid morning," he said. He spread his arms palms upward, as though to embrace the beauty of the day.

Alyssa looked at Diego without emotion and pulled her mother closer to her. Huddled together, they continued past him down the sidewalk. Diego turned and walked with them. "Are you both doing alright? Is there anything you need?"

Alyssa's silence didn't deter Diego's attempts to engage her in conversation. "I know times are difficult," he said. "Unfortunately, that's the way with change. You must realize that the world has always been that way. Nothing ever stays the same. If one is to live a happy life, one must be ready to accept that tomorrow's world may be different from today's. And I do want you to be happy, Alyssa. Please understand that...more than anything, I wish for that."

Alyssa stopped. "If you truly mean what you say, Diego, "have my father released from prison. Only then can I ever be happy again."

Diego stepped close to her. "I'll try, Alyssa," he said, "if you will."

Alyssa blinked. "Do you mean it, Diego? Could you really do it?"

"I can try. The charges against your father were very serious. If I hadn't intervened, he certainly would have been shot. Others have been executed for much less."

"Don't make me laugh, Diego. They were only trumped-up charges. You know he did nothing wrong. My father's a good man. He's guilty only of trying to lessen the harm done to people by Batista."

"He was tried and convicted," Diego said. "That can't be changed. I can only plead that it would be in the best interests of Cuba for him to return to his family. It will be a risk for me to even try, but if I thought there was a future for us, Alyssa, I'd be willing to make the attempt. Will you at least consider it?"

Alyssa took her eyes from Diego and looked to the bright, blue sky behind him. A single white cloud moved slowly across it. Roberto was gone to the United States. There was little hope of ever seeing him again. As much as she detested Diego, perhaps there really was a possibility that he could free her father. It would only require her to sacrifice herself. She could do it if she must. "Alright, Diego," she heard herself say, "I'll think about it."

29

Colonel Alfredo Gomez clasped his hands behind his head and rocked back in the big leather chair. He raised his legs onto the mahogany desk, surveyed his surroundings and reviewed his position. Here I am, he thought, an important man sitting in my new office. Finally, I have what I deserve. This is what I've worked my entire life to achieve.

As Minister of Prisons, I will first take a tour of the penal system. There are many prisons because the new regime has many enemies. Many Batista supporters fled the country. Many others were tried and executed, but thousands more have been sentenced to prison. I smile to think of the many opportunities my new position will bring me. Men in prison are desperate and desperate men are eager to improve their lot. Many of the incarcerated are from wealthy families whose relatives managed to abscond with their fortunes when they escaped from the island. A prisoner with rich relations can make for a lucrative proposition. Yes, the possibilities to take good advantage of this new responsibility appear endless.

And the women. Surely there will be many opportunities for women. Just think of that fat girl in Santa Fe whom I routinely bedded so many years ago. Why did the stupid girl go and kill herself? Such a waste. I can make no sense of it, even now. I suppose some people just don't know how to be happy. Fortunately, I do…I most certainly do.

A loud rapping on the door of his office interrupted Gomez's planning. Before he could respond, the door was thrown open. He swung his boots to the floor and jumped to his feet. Who had the nerve to enter without his permission?

A tall man in an expensive suit strode into the room, confident in his own authority. "*Señor* Montalvo," Gomez said, reaching out his hand. "What an extreme pleasure!"

Diego smiled as he took the outstretched hand. "Colonel Gomez."

Gomez gestured to a chair near his desk. "Please, *seño*r Montalvo, do make yourself comfortable."

"*Gracias*," Diego said. He looked around the room and nodded his approval. "Are you happy with your new office, Colonel Gomez?"

"Oh, *sí*!" Gomez said. "I'm very happy. The office is very nice. I'm certain I'll be able to do very good work here."

"*Bueno*," Diego said. "I'm pleased to hear that, and I know Fidel will be happy to hear that, as well."

Gomez smiled. It felt good to be positioned so near to the seat of power. Diego Montalvo came from an old and respected family. True, the purpose of the revolution was to cast off the domination of the wealthy, but one couldn't help but be impressed, as well as intimidated, by those from privileged backgrounds. Diego Montalvo was close to Castro and had responsibility for many civil appointments. He had found this position for Gomez upon Castro's order. "To what do I owe this distinguished visit from Fidel Castro's personal attorney?" Gomez asked.

"I've come to ask a favor of you," Diego said. "The father of a very dear friend of mine is in one of your prisons. He was an important functionary in Batista's government. When the revolution was successful, he was jailed and tried for crimes against the people. He was found guilty and sentenced to life imprisonment."

Gomez listened without interruption. He'd only been in his new job a couple of hours and already a great opportunity was presenting itself. If he could do a favor for Diego Montalvo, it could be very beneficial to his future.

"I don't take issue with the decision to imprison the man," Diego said. "He must pay for his crimes, of course. I only wonder if he might be able to pay his debt to society in the sunshine. I ask you to see if he might be transferred to a facility where he can serve his time by working outside. He's currently in a prison cell, which is very upsetting to my friend and her mother."

"*Sí, señor* Montalvo," Gomez said. "As you know, I'm new in this position and don't know what other facilities might be available, but I'll make it my first priority to find out immediately. If it's your wish that the man be transferred, then you may consider it done."

"I knew I could count on you," Diego said. "When El Comandante told me how you kept the federal troops away while he marched on Havana, I knew that you must be a dependable man. When he told me that we needed a man such as yourself in a position of authority, I immediately thought of this situation, where the responsibilities are great." In truth, Diego recalled, when Gomez contacted Castro and reminded him of his service to the revolution, Castro had instructed Diego to find Gomez a job where his ambition for power would allow him to be manipulated whenever necessary.

"He's a man who can be trusted to do whatever is in his own self-interest," Castro had said. "Find him a position where he can be *useful*."

"What is the name of this prisoner?" Gomez said.

"Hernando Villanueva. He was a colonel under Batista."

Gomez nearly gasped aloud when he heard the name of his old benefactor but caught himself and maintained his composure. "And where is this man now?"

"Near Havana…in Matanzas prison."

"I'll go there at once and see what can be done," Gomez said.

Diego rose from his chair. "*Bueno*! Then my business here is concluded. It's good to know that we have a Minister of Prisons who can be relied upon. Please let me know what arrangements you've been able to make. *Adios*, Colonel Gomez."

"*Adios, señor* Montalvo," Gomez said. "I'm certain I'll be getting back to you soon with a good report."

Gomez called for his driver. "Take me to Matanzas Prison," he ordered the corporal. As they rode, Gomez thought about his recent conversation with Diego Montalvo. Diego had indicated that the concerned party was Villanueva's daughter and that she was "a dear friend." He could only be talking about the little girl Gomez had saved from the big wave. Yes, she would be grown up now and about Diego's age. Very interesting. Such a connection would be useful in his future dealings with Diego.

The corporal opened the car door and Colonel Gomez exited with a stern countenance and a purposeful stride. He inspected the operation as he entered Matanzas Prison. His eyes darted right and left, and he returned the hurried salutes of the attending guards with perfunctory salutes of his own. His outer demeanor was stiff and official, but inside he was glowing with the respect his new position was giving him.

The commanding officer leaped to his feet and saluted when Gomez burst into his office. "You have a Colonel Hernando Villanueva here?"

"*Sí*, Colonel."

"I want to see him," Gomez said.

"*Sí*, Colonel, *sí*." The officer grabbed a riding crop and strode to the door. "I'll take you to him." He signaled a guard to accompany them.

Gomez enjoyed the sound made by his boot heels as he followed the commanding officer down the prison hallway. They passed beneath flickering light bulbs. The floors and walls were wet from the dripping of water pipes. From all sides came the moans of desperate men. Gomez raised a gloved hand to his nose to diminish the nauseating odors. Rats scurried into the shadows.

The guard stopped in front of a cell near the end of the hallway. "This is the prisoner, Villanueva."

Gomez looked through a small opening in the wooden cell door. All was dark… he could see nothing. The guard gave him a flashlight and Gomez shined it into the cell. An old man in a gray prison uniform lay on a bare cot and stared at the ceiling. On the floor next to the cot was an uneaten bowl of watery beans. In the middle of the beans was a single cube of pig fat.

The guard opened the cell door and stood back. "*Attencion*! The Minister of Prisons is here to see you. Stand at attention!"

Villanueva rolled his head toward the noise outside his cell. There was always noise. His legs were stiff. He swung them around and sat up on the edge of his cot. Two uniformed men stood in the doorway.

30

Hialeah, Florida

Magner leaned on the clubhouse rail at Hialeah Park as the thoroughbreds worked out. He inhaled the chilly, early-morning smell of the track. Steam rose from the droppings of the horses and from the infield lake. Through the fog, flamingos grouped together on the island. They formed a pink contrast against the green of the grass and reflected in the blue of the lake. Horses thudded past. He loved it. Back inside the clubhouse, he helped himself to a buffet breakfast of scrambled eggs, bacon, and hot coffee, while he studied the *Daily Racing Form*. He went through each of the twelve races and reviewed the entries. By late morning, he'd made his decisions on all the day's races except the feature race, the Flamingo Stakes. Bally Ache, a good-looking horse who'd won five two-year-old stakes races the previous year or Victoria Park, the Canadian horse who'd beaten Bally Ache in February? He didn't have to decide now. He'd get a drink and think about it.

Magner folded his *Racing Form* and moved to the bar that swept around one corner of the first floor of the clubhouse. "Bloody Mary," he told the bartender.

"You got it, Mac."

The warm-up period out on the track had ended. Through the round window behind the bar, Magner saw the tractor go past, grooming the track for the first race. The room began to crowd. He left some money on the bar and took his drink out behind the clubhouse to the paddock area where he surveyed the Flamingo Day women in pink dresses and hats. Then he walked over to the horse path that ran from the paddock out through the tunnel under the grandstand to the track. A guard in a white uniform and white gloves held back crossing pedestrian traffic while the last of the exercise riders came off the track and headed back to the barns.

On the other side of the path, standing well back from the passing horses, was a young man in the traditional white pants and shirt of Hialeah employees. On the breast pocket of his shirt was an embroidered pink flamingo. He pushed an orange, steel cart loaded with glass jugs of water. Magner blinked. It was the young Cuban, Roberto, from the *Criollo*.

After the horses had passed, Roberto pushed the cart across the horse path from the grandstand to the clubhouse side. The water bottles jiggled and clinked.

"I can see why you keep the cart so far back from the horses," Magner said, "that cart makes quite a racket." He bit off a piece of celery stalk from his drink and grinned. "What gives?"

Roberto looked into the eyes of the red-haired man holding a Bloody Mary. "*Señor* Magner!"

Magner motioned to an umbrella-shaded table away from the crowd. "Let's go sit over there," he said.

"But the water…"

"Forget the fuckin' water. Nobody around here looks like they're dying of thirst, or anything else for that matter." He tucked his newspaper under the arm that held his drink. He draped the other around Roberto's shoulders and steered him to the table.

"So, what the hell are you doing *here*?" Magner said.

"How long has it been since I last saw you?" Roberto said. "Two years? A lot has happened. After Castro took over, things were bad in Cuba. They arrested my girlfriend's father and sentenced him to life in prison. We escaped Cuba in my father's boat. She was supposed to come with us, but she didn't show up at the dock. I guess she thought she needed to stay and try to help her father. Many people were killed. My mother died on the trip over."

"I'm sorry," Magner said.

"We got lost, but the Coast Guard picked us up and took us to Key West. Then we came up here. My father's working for a company making cigars and José's father has a job as a mechanic.

José and I are on the maintenance crew here at the track, but the racing season is ending soon. So…that's it."

"Sounds bad," Magner said. "That whole mess down there in Cuba really pisses me off."

"Nothing we can do about it," Roberto said. "How was your racing in the SORC this year?"

"We just got back from the Bahamas. We won a few races, but a boat called *Solution* won the overall cup. We'll get 'em next year."

Roberto looked at his cart. "Well," he said, "it was nice seeing you Mr. Magner, but I'd better get moving. My job here will be ending even sooner if I don't get these water bottles delivered."

Magner leaned forward over the table. "Listen," he said, "I've got something a lot bigger for you guys…trust me…a *lot* bigger."

Roberto looked across the table and tried to analyze Magner. He must be important. The way he'd handled Carlos's brush with the law in St. Petersburg had shown that. He seemed to know things. "'Bigger?'"

Magner spread the *Racing Form* out on the table. "We'll talk about it later," he said. "First, help me with the Flamingo. I can't decide between Bally Ache and Victoria Park."

Roberto shook his head. Life was crazy. A few minutes ago, he was delivering water. Now he was being asked by one of the most mysterious and influential men in the place to help him pick a horse. "I watched those horses race against each other earlier this season," he said. "Victoria Park is very fast. He set a new track record by almost two seconds. But that race was only a mile and a sixteenth. The Flamingo is longer by half a furlong, and I think that extra distance might be what Bally Ache needs."

"You've been paying attention," Magner said.

Roberto shrugged. "I'm here. It's a horse track."

Magner got up from the table. "We'll talk about that later. Right now, I'm going to get some money down on Bally Ache. I'll meet you and José in the clubhouse bar after the races. Okay?"

"Okay," Roberto said. "We'll be there."

"You might as well turn in your uniforms and keys," Magner said. "You won't be coming back here after today."

Roberto and José went to the clubhouse bar at the end of the day. An exultant Magner was holding forth on a bar stool. There was a pretty woman with a floppy, pink hat nestled in the crook of one arm and a small crowd gathered around him. Magner saw the Cubans enter and waved them over. "My personal handicapper," he said. He released the woman and slapped Roberto on the back. "What'll you have boys?"

"Just a beer for me," Roberto said.

José nodded. "A beer for me, too."

"Two beers and another Johnny Walker Black, my good man," Magner said to the bartender. He sounded drunk.

The drinks arrived and Magner led the boys to a corner table. He raised his glass, "To Bally Ache." Then, in a low whisper, he said, "Castro's spies are everywhere."

Roberto began to understand Magner's obnoxious inebriation to be a ruse.

"He sure looked good today, didn't he?" Magner said. "Got his revenge on that speedy Canadian son-of-a-bitch!" His talk was loud and drunken, but he interspersed it with whispered phrases. "We're going to overthrow Castro. Sending in an advance group of infiltrators. Top-secret operation. Meet me tomorrow night. Eight o'clock. Bring a bag, you may be gone a while." Magner pulled out his wallet and left enough money on the table to cover the bill and the tip. At the same time, he slid a white business card across the table to Roberto. Then he stood up, bid everyone a loud, "Adieu," and wove unsteadily out of the bar.

Roberto covered the card Magner had slid to him with one hand and took a quick look around the room. Then he peeked at the card under a couple of raised fingers. Beneath the picture of a freighter were the words *"Gibraltar Steamship Corporation"* and the address.

31

"Who are you?" Villanueva said when Gomez and the officer entered his cell.

"Stand up!" the officer shouted. He moved toward the old man and raised his riding crop. "Stand up when El Colonel addresses you!"

Gomez raised a hand. "Stop," he said. "Leave us."

The officer looked from one to the other. "*Sí*, Colonel," he said and backed out of the cell.

Gomez sat at one end of the cot. "Do you remember me?" he said.

Villanueva looked at Gomez's face and shook his head. "There's not much that I care to remember any more."

"I'm Colonel Gomez. I was Corporal Gomez before I saved your daughter from drowning, and you had me promoted to Sergeant. Then, when I brought you the treasure chest, you recommended me for the *Academia Militar*. I passed all the entrance examinations and was accepted. After I graduated, I rose to the rank of captain in Batista's army. When Castro came into power, he made me a colonel and appointed me Minister of Prisons."

The light bulb in the hallway provided dim illumination through the open door of the cell. The old man looked at Gomez again and a look of recognition began to come over his face. "*Sí*," Villanueva said. "*Sí*, I *do* remember you, now. You're the one who came to our summer house in Santa Fe."

"*Sí! Sí!*" Gomez said. If the old man remembered that much, he might be able to remember more.

"And you're now a *colonel*?" Villanueva said.

"*Sí! Sí!* I'm a colonel. Believe me, *señor*, I'm as amazed at that development as you are. Life is curious, is it not? Once you were a colonel and I was a nobody. Now, I'm a colonel and you're a nobody." Gomez laughed at the irony.

The old man shook his head and looked away. Life wasn't curious. It was cruel. What sense did it make for a weasel such as this Gomez to have an important position and he be locked away? God liked to play his games.

Gomez stopped laughing. "So, you look at me with distaste, eh? The fact remains that when our conversation is finished, I'll be leaving this place, and you will still be here. Now tell me, where's the treasure?"

"I don't know," Villanueva said.

"What did you do with it?"

"I don't have it."

"You didn't give it to Batista!?" Gomez said. "You said you'd never do that. You said that it belonged to the people!"

"No, I didn't give it to Batista."

"Then where is it?"

"I don't know."

"I see," Gomez said. "You know where it is, but you're not going to tell me."

"I don't know where it is."

"You know," Gomez said, "such riches could be of very important benefit to both of us. Besides, the revolution was for the people. Castro represents them, now. It's time to give them their treasure."

Villanueva swung his gray mane around to face Gomez. "Castro doesn't represent the people! He's a dictator!"

"Ssshhh," Gomez said. "Not so loud. I'm here to help you, but if you're not careful, you'll get yourself into even more trouble. Look, you helped me, so I'll help you. I'm going to have you transferred to a work prison, where you can be outdoors. The fresh air will clear your head. Then I'll come see you again and you'll be more reasonable."

"I doubt it," Villanueva said. "I'm telling you the truth when I say I don't know where the treasure is."

"We'll see," Gomez said. He rose from the cot and walked out of the cell. He closed the door behind him and looked back through the peephole at Villanueva. "We'll see," he said again.

"I've managed to have your father transferred out of Matanzas Prison to a work camp," Diego said. "Now he can be outside in the fresh air."

"You have?" Alyssa said. They were sitting on the veranda of the guesthouse. "Thank you, Diego. That's wonderful. Where is he?"

"Las Canteras de Miranda. Near Santiago de Cuba."

"Santiago de Cuba! But that's a thousand kilometers from here!"

"I know," Diego said, "but it's the best place for him. I want you to be pleased, Alyssa."

"I believe you do, Diego," she said, "but it will be hard for me to see him."

"Yes," Diego said. As far as he was concerned, the further her father was away from her, the better. He hoped that out of sight would mean out of mind and reduce her father's influence over her. If she stopped worrying about her father, she might be more cooperative with him. "We must think of what is best for your father," he said.

"Of course, you're right," Alyssa said. "Thank you, Diego, for your kindness."

"You're welcome. I want to do everything I can to make you happy, because you know that I love you, Alyssa."

"Yes," she said. "I know."

"I've been thinking," Diego said. "If we were married, then your father would be my father-in-law. I believe that my having such a relationship with your father might carry some weight with Fidel. I might even be able to convince El Commandante to have your father freed from prison." Diego stopped for a moment to let his words sink in. Then he posed the question she'd been dreading. "Will you marry me, Alyssa?"

She looked at Diego. It was inevitable that one day this moment would arrive and now it had. It was a dread she'd harbored since the day they'd first moved into his guesthouse. Marry him? She looked at his hands...the thought of those long fingers moving across her body made her feel sick. She could taste the bile rising at the back of her throat and she thought she might vomit. Her skin crawled and a cold feeling spread through her. Oh, Roberto, she thought. You are my one and only love. I will love you forever. Only and always you. Always only you. Please forgive me, my darling, because I have no choice if it means my father can be free. I must do it. I cannot *not* do it.

She looked away and took a deep breath. "Alright, Diego" she said. "I'll marry you." As she said the words, she felt her heart slide out of her and heavy sadness move in to take its place.

32

It had been dark for two hours when José's father dropped them off at the Gibraltar Steamship Corporation. "Should I wait for you?" Enrique said.

"I don't think so," Roberto said. "We'll call you when we know more about what's going on."

Chip Magner was sitting in a black Ford when they arrived. He got out of the car and motioned for Roberto and José to follow him. He led them through a side door of the building and down a hallway to an office. "Have a seat, gentlemen and I'll explain how you fit in to all of this."

Roberto and José took seats across from each other. They'd talked of nothing else since running into Magner at Hialeah. "Who *is* this guy, anyway?" From the room next door, they could hear a voice talking loudly in Spanish. The speaker was ranting about Cuba and Castro. It dawned on them that it was a radio broadcast to Cuba.

"Okay," Magner said, "here's the story. There're a lot of people here from Cuba, as well as back on the island, who want Castro out. I assume you guys feel the same way?"

Roberto and José both nodded. "Castro has betrayed the revolution," Roberto said. "When he first took over, everyone was behind him. He could've done great things, but he's gotten lost in his own rhetoric."

"Good," Magner said. "There's a guy on Miami Beach who's willing to finance an infiltration. What we need to start with are radio operators who can be slipped onto the island to keep us abreast of what's going on. At the same time, we'll be training volunteers to infiltrate into Cuba. The infiltrators will coordinate with rebel forces which are already being formed on the island."

"We want to do something," Roberto said, "but, we're not radio operators."

"No problem," Magner said. "We'll teach you."

Roberto and José looked at each other. "Okay."

"Alright, let's go. I've got a boat waiting to take you to a little island on the Gulf Coast of Florida where your training will begin. You're gonna love it." They walked out to Magner's Ford. "Oh, by the way," he said, "you understand, of course, that if you're caught when you get to Cuba, you'll be shot as spies."

Magner turned west and soon they were speeding through the night on the Tamiami Trail, the two-lane highway that ran through the Everglades to Tampa on the Gulf Coast. "What's your involvement in all of this?" Roberto said.

Magner grinned. His face and teeth were illumined by the light from the car's gauges. "Let's just say that I like to lend a hand where it's needed."

Roberto got the message that there was no point asking any more questions. Whatever Magner was, he wasn't about to reveal it to them.

When they reached Ft. Meyers, he turned down a private road that wound through patches of mangrove until they reached the water. A boat was tied to an old wooden dock. "This is where we say goodbye," Magner said. "The man on the boat goes by 'Bob'. He'll take you out to Useppa Island, where you'll begin your training. Good luck. I'll be seeing you again before you leave the States."

They'd been on Useppa Island two weeks and new recruits were coming in every day. "Must be about twenty of us here now," Roberto said.

"Yes, and a lot of Americans doing the training," José said.

"Funny thing about the Americans," Roberto said. "They all seem to have military connections."

Freddie Gould, the millionaire from Miami Beach, who Magner had said was financing the infiltration, showed up one day. "Get a look at that guy," Roberto said. "No way, he can be paying for all of this…no way. Somebody's bullshitting us. Look at all these American professionals around here. You know what I think? I think this is a CIA operation."

"I think you're right," José said. "Of course, I don't know when you've had time to figure all this out."

"What do you mean, Amigo?"

"I mean that since we left Cuba you've only been thinking about one thing…and that one thing is Alyssa. When you were at Hialeah pushing water bottles, your mind was someplace else, and I knew it was Alyssa. When you were delivering the linens, your mind was someplace else, and I knew it was Alyssa. And I know the number one reason you want to go back to Cuba is to see her."

Roberto nodded. "You're very perceptive, my friend. I think of nothing else."

33

"Diego has changed, Mami," Alyssa said, as she painted her mother's fingernails. "Since we've been married, he's become almost conspiratorial with me. He shares intimate knowledge of Castro's inner workings. He's telling me things that he shouldn't, but he wants me to know how important he is." She sat back, "There, nails all done, let's go for our walk."

As they walked along the street, a black sedan pulled near to the curb. A voice called out from inside the car. "Alyssa, *hola*. It's me. How're you doing?"

The voice was a familiar one and Alyssa bent to peer inside. The old man in the car pulled a false white beard away from his face. "Francisco!" she said. "What are you doing here? I haven't seen you since the university. Somebody told me you're wanted by the government for subversion. They say you've been speaking out against Castro and printing anti-Castro pamphlets."

"Never mind that. I must talk to you," Francisco said. "When can I see you?"

Alyssa shrank away…it could be dangerous. If Diego found out she'd talked to Francisco, they'd both be in trouble. "I don't know, Francisco. What could you want to talk to me about?"

"I can't tell you now. Just trust me that it's important or I wouldn't bother you."

Diego was leaving the next day on government business to another part of the island. He'd be gone for a few days, so that could be a good opportunity. She did admire Francisco for his resistance efforts against Castro and it was intriguing that he wanted to speak with her. "Okay," she said into the car. "Meet me here at ten o'clock tomorrow night. I'll be able to talk to you then."

"I'll be here," Francisco said.

The next night, after Diego had gone off on his business trip, Alyssa put her mother in bed for the night and walked out of the house and along the street to the curb where she'd last seen Francisco. A few minutes after ten o'clock, the black sedan drove up and the passenger door swung open. Alyssa slipped inside and the car continued down the street.

"Francisco," Alyssa said, "it's very dangerous for you to come here. Do you know who my husband is?"

"Yes, I do know who your husband is," Francisco said. "That's why I've come to see you. Everyone knows why you married Diego Montalvo. We know you and we know you could never be a *Fidelista*. You married him to protect your parents. This much is obvious. Tell me if this is not so."

Alyssa leaned her head back against the seat of the car and looked out through the windshield into the dark night in front of her. "*Sí*, it is so," she said. "You do know me, Francisco."

"So, will you help us?" he said.

"Help you? What can I do to help you?"

"You can get information for us. What plans are being made by Castro? Who among us has been discovered and may soon be arrested? What is the strength of his military? What weapons has he gotten from the Russians? Everything's important for us to know."

A spy! How exciting! Castro and Diego had taken everything from her. They'd imprisoned her father and taken their home, which had driven her mother insane. Because of Castro, Roberto and José had had to flee the country. She loathed Diego for manipulating her into marrying him and she hated his precious 'Commandante'. Getting information for the underground movement was the perfect way for her to get revenge against them both. "Yes, Francisco," she said. "I'm eager to do anything I can to help you."

Francisco gave her a small camera and several rolls of film. "Take pictures of any important looking papers that you see," he said. "And keep your ears open. We'll arrange to make periodic contact with you."

When Alyssa returned home that evening she went into Diego's study and began looking through the papers on his desk. It all looked important, so she took pictures of everything. She wondered if he would have her shot if he found her out. Probably. I guess I should also start going to those parties and functions he always wants me to attend with him. She couldn't stand being around those people, but it might be a good chance to get information.

The next time Diego asked her to accompany him to an official function, she acquiesced. "Okay, Diego, I'll go with you."

"You will? That would be wonderful, Alyssa. It will make me proud to walk in with you on my arm. I'll be the envy of every man in the room. There will be many very important people there. Maybe even El Commandanté, himself."

How delightful, thought Alyssa. Just who I want to see. Too bad I don't have some poison I could put in his drink.

Castro was not at the party, but many other people in his government were. There were even a few Russians. It was almost too good to be true. The drunker they got, the more they opened up. Everyone wanted to impress her with their importance and what they knew.

She heard a voice at her elbow. "*Buenos noches, señora,* you're here alone?"

Alyssa turned to see a man dressed in a military uniform. "No," she said. "That's my husband over there, talking business. It's not interesting to me."

"Ah, s*eñor* Montalvo," said the man. "I'll keep you company while he's engaged in his conversation. I'm Captain Rodriguez. At your service, s*eñora,*" he said with a slight bow.

"Oh, thank you, Captain. I thought I was going to die of boredom. What a handsome uniform! What do you do?"

"*Gracias*, s*eñora*. I'm an explosives expert. I'm in command of the munitions depot just outside Havana."

"Really!" Alyssa said. "It sounds so exciting – blowing things up."

"Yes, but it's very dangerous," Captain Rodriguez said. "Only the bravest of men are chosen to work with explosives."

"Then you must be very brave *and* very smart," Alyssa said, "because you're in charge."

Rodriguez beamed and rocked up on his toes in response to her admiration.

"How do you make things blow up? Do you light a fuse and then run away like with a firecracker?"

Rodriguez laughed. "No, *señora*, that was the old days. Now we use plastic explosives and detonate them with an electric charge."

"Really?" Alyssa said. "It sounds spectacular. I'd love to see it sometime."

"Would you? If you like, I could get you a pass to come out to the range and show you how everything works."

"I would just *love* that," Alyssa said. "How exciting!"

Several days later, Alyssa took the biggest purse she had and drove Enrique's red convertible out to the blasting range. The guard at the gate carefully examined her pass before letting her onto the grounds. It seemed strange to him that such an attractive woman would be coming there.

"*Señora* Montalvo!" Captain Rodriguez said when she was announced at his office. He held a chair for her. "I've been anticipating your visit. How good of you to come."

Alyssa smiled at him. "Thank you, Captain Rodriguez," she said, "we must be very careful that my husband doesn't find out that I've been here. He's a very jealous man."

Rodriguez's eyes widened. Diego Montalvo was dangerous. He knew he was playing with fire, but to hell with it. He'd take the chance. This woman was too intoxicating to resist. "Oh, *sí, sí*," he said. "We'll be very careful. It will be our little secret." He winked.

"Thank you," Alyssa said.

"Come, *Señora,* let me take you out the munitions shed, I'll show you how explosives work." Inside the shed, he began by showing her stacks of dynamite.

"You still use dynamite?" Alyssa said. "You told me you didn't light fuses anymore."

"Dynamite is still used," Captain Rodriguez said, "but we use timing devices or an electrical charge to ignite it."

Alyssa pointed to some piles of small, wrapped bricks. "What's that?" she said.

"That's C-3. It's a very powerful plastic explosive. It can be easily attached to anything that you want to destroy." The captain picked up a package of the explosives and tossed it in his hand.

Alyssa backed away and Rodriquez laughed. "Oh, no," he said, "it can't explode without a detonating device, like this…a blasting cap." He showed her a small tube connected to a wire. "The Russians gave this stuff to us. The C-3 gets brittle in cold temperatures, so they have little use for it."

"I'd like to see a timer," Alyssa said.

Rodriguez smiled. The location of the timers would lead them deeper inside the shed. "They're just over here," he said. "Follow me."

Alyssa followed him. As she passed the stacks of C-3, she slipped as many of them into her purse as she thought she could carry, along with a matching supply of detonating caps.

When they reached the timers, Alyssa listened as Captain Rodriguez described their operation. When he finished, he turned to Alyssa. His eyes narrowed, his face became serious, and he took a step towards her.

Alyssa looked at her watch. "My, my, look how the time has just flown," she said. "Everything's been so interesting, but I'm afraid I must go before my husband gets home. Thank you so much for your hospitality, Captain."   She turned and walked rapidly out of the shed the way that they'd entered. She had what she'd come for. Francisco would be pleased.

Rodriguez trailed along behind her. "I hope that I'll be seeing you again soon," he said.

"Yes, Captain," Alyssa called back over her shoulder. "I'll try to arrange it. *Gracías. adios.*"

Alyssa was still flushed with the elation of her success when she drove back through the guard gate of the ammunition depot. The guard smiled and nodded as she passed. Now he understood her reason for being here. A rendezvous. Why else?

Alyssa had driven around the first bend in the road and was out of sight of the blasting range when her body began to shake. She pulled to the side of the road and put the car into Park, while she trembled. Relax, relax, she told herself…take some deep breaths. She patted her face and began to feel better …this espionage stuff was thrilling, but it took its toll on one's physiology.

34

When Chip Magner showed up on Useppa Island. Roberto and José pulled him aside. "You must tell us," José said. "Who's really behind all this? We know it's not Freddie Gould."

Magner frowned. "Unfortunately," he said, "this is a secret that's not being kept very well. You're right, there's support for this operation at very high levels within the United States government. But really, that's all that I can tell you right now."

"CIA?" José said.

"That's *all* I can tell you," Magner said. "Now, the reason I'm here is that you guys might be more help to the success of the operation if we take advantage of your military training."

"How would you do that?" Roberto said.

"This thing is evolving into something quite a bit bigger than the original plan, which was a simple infiltration. It's starting to look more like a small-scale invasion, and we'll need trained naval officers to lead the amphibious assault. The problem is that planning for this venture is way ahead of financing and the whole operation may fail for lack of money before it even gets off the ground."

"No money?" Roberto said. He and José looked at each other. They each remembered the night they'd stored the treasure chest of emeralds in the keel of the *Criollo*.

"Are you thinking what I'm thinking?" José said.

"Yes, Amigo, I am. We were told that it was to be used 'for the Cuban people' and I'd say that this qualifies." Roberto turned back to Magner. "We may be able to help with the financing," he said.

Magner chuckled. "Well," he said, "you probably don't understand what an operation like this costs. I'm not talking nickels and dimes here. I'm talking about *a lot* of money."

"So are we," José said.

"No kidding?"

"The problem is that it's still in Cuba," Roberto said.

"If I can get you over there, can you get it back here?"

Roberto nodded. "Why not? You get us in there. We'll find our way back."

"You realize of course," Magner said, "that you could still be shot as spies if you're caught."

José laughed. "Actually, they could shoot us twice. Once for being spies and once for desertion from the Cuban Navy."

"That brings up a good point, Amigo," Roberto said. "There's not much sense in both of us going back. It would only take one of us to get it. If the other one stayed here, he could continue training."

"That's true," Magner said. "We're going to be moving the whole group in a couple of days. If one of you stays here, you can begin assuming your leadership role for the invasion."

"I guess that makes sense," José said. "But how will we decide who goes and who stays?"

"I'll go," Roberto said. "I *have* to go."

"Okay," José said. "You go. And give my cousin a kiss for me."

"I know what you and José are up to," Ernesto said. "There're a lot of rumors about a Cuban force being raised to take Cuba back from Castro. I've also heard that an American who calls himself 'Eduardo' is throwing a lot of money around looking for somebody to take over when Castro is gone."

"I can't tell you what I'm doing," Roberto said. "Nobody should be saying anything about anything."

"Just be careful, Machito," Ernesto said. "I don't want it to be just Tomo and me."

"I promise that I'll be careful, Papi. Everything will be fine."

Roberto again met Magner at the offices of the Gibraltar Steamship Corporation, as they had agreed, at 8 o'clock in the evening. This time, however, when they got in the car, Magner turned south on U.S. 1. Magner stopped to fill up the Ford with gas before they got onto the Overseas Highway. "There's not going to be much open between here and Key West at this time of night," he said.

Four hours later, Magner turned off the road at a sign that said, "Safe Harbor Marina." At the marina entrance, they were stopped by sheriff's deputies. Magner reached his arm out the car window and flipped open his wallet. One of the deputies examined Magner's ID and waved them through.

They parked and Roberto followed Magner through the darkness and down a long dock to a waiting speedboat. He took note of the name painted on the stern of the boat – "*Riffer*." Magner introduced him to the driver. "Musculito will get you there, but you'll have to find your own way back. If you can make it to Guantanamo Bay Naval Base, we'll send a plane to pick you up."

Roberto threw his bag in the boat. "Okay," he said. "Are you ready, Musculito?"

"*Sí*," said the boatman. "I'll take you to Arcos de Cannas, where La Habana and Matanzas provinces meet."

"*Bueno*," Roberto said, "I know that area well."

"I'll stand offshore until a rowboat comes out to get you. When you land on the beach, you'll be met by Jorge Fundora. He'll get you inland. You must move quickly and quietly. We're all risking our lives."

"I understand," Roberto said.

"Okay, then, let's go," Musculito said.

Magner handed Roberto a wallet and a sealed envelope. "The wallet has money and false identification. You'll be met by Jorge Fundora. The envelope you're to give to Erancisco who'll be your connection in Havana. Good luck, I'll be waiting to hear from you."

"You will."

Musculito started the big V-20 engine of the *Riffer* and turned on the running lights. They motored slowly out of the harbor, away from the shore lights and out into the darkness of the Straits of Florida. Roberto looked back toward shore and remembered when they'd first been brought to Key West by the Coast Guard. He looked back out to the blackness in front of him with its backlighting of a million stars and thought of his mother. Her body was somewhere down in the dark depths below them, and her soul was somewhere up there among the stars. A great sadness came into his chest. He turned away from Musculito and brushed the tears from his face.

When they were out of the channel, Musculito shoved the throttle lever all the way forward. The engine roared, the boat rose high in the water, and they accelerated out into the darkness. Soon, they were crashing through the chop of the Gulf Stream. When they reached the calm water on the Cuban side of the Gulf Stream, Musculito doused the *Riffer's* running lights. Roberto could see lights on shore and his heart beat quickly with the excitement of returning to the island and the hope of seeing Alyssa again. They continued to race through the water at high speed, paralleling the Cuban coastline. Then Musculito cut the motor back to an idle. The boat relaxed down into the water, and they cruised in toward shore. It had taken them less than two hours in the speedboat.

Musculito began to flash a light as a signal to those waiting on shore. There were answering flashes, and a small rowboat began to move out toward them. Musculito scanned the sea around them for patrol boats. When the rowboat arrived, Roberto was surprised to find the boatman wearing only his underwear. Roberto stepped out of the *Riffer* and dropped down into the rowboat. The rower nodded and headed back to shore with quick silent strokes.

Jorge Fundora was there to greet him. "Come quickly," he said. "We'll get you to a safe house." Roberto turned to thank the half-naked boatman, but he'd disappeared.

35

Dawn was breaking when Roberto and Jorge arrived at the safe house in Havana. Jorge introduced him to Francisco. "You have an envelope for me?" Francisco said.

"*Sí.*" Roberto handed him the envelope Magner had given him.

Francisco opened it and read the contents. He looked up at Roberto and smiled. "There are no instructions here. It only says we're to get you to wherever you want to go."

"My work is here in Havana," Roberto said. "When my work is done, I'll need to get to Guantanamo Bay."

"We can arrange that," Francisco said.

Roberto slept in a back-bedroom most of the day. When darkness came, he slipped out of the safe house and made his way to his sister's house. Before he did anything else, he wanted to find out about Alyssa. A baseball cap was his only disguise. He stayed in the shadows and hoped he wouldn't see anyone who could recognize him. He breathed the old smells, the honeysuckle that climbed along the fences and the aromas of familiar foods coming from open windows.

When Roberto reached Maria's house, he stood in the shadow of a banyan tree and tried to see what was happening inside. He saw only Maria. When he was satisfied that her husband wasn't home, he stole around to the back of the house. "Maria," he whispered through the open window.

Maria was standing at the kitchen sink, washing dishes. She was lost in her own thoughts but looked up when she heard her name. Had she really heard someone? Then, she heard her name again.

"Maria, it's me – Roberto."

She leaned forward over the sink and shielded her eyes from the light inside the house. Roberto's face came out of the darkness. He put a finger to his lips. "*Dios, mio*," she said. "My God, Roberto!" She turned off the light in the kitchen and opened the back door. He slipped inside and closed the door behind him. They embraced until Maria remembered the danger of his being there. She pulled away enough to see his face. "Roberto, what are you doing here? If they find you, they'll kill you."

"I know," Roberto said, "but there are some things I must do. Where are your children?"

"Asleep."

"And your husband?"

"He'll not return soon. He's at a party meeting."

"A party meeting?"

"*Sí*, the communist party. They have meetings to talk about what everyone should be doing and then they snitch on anybody that doesn't follow along. If any of them knew you were here, they'd turn you in to the authorities in hopes of receiving favor from the party. Tell me, Roberto, how are Mami and Papi?"

Roberto hadn't thought about having to answer this question. He'd forgotten Maria didn't know about their mother's death and he decided not to tell her now. The news would devastate her. She'd be so distraught that it could lead to his being discovered and he couldn't risk that. There was too much riding on the success of his mission. "They're all fine," he said.

"Sometimes I wish I'd gone with you," she said. "This is no longer our country, Roberto. It's only Fidel's country."

"How is Alyssa?"

Maria hesitated. "I'm sorry, Roberto, but if you've come for her, I'm afraid you're too late."

"Too late?" A thousand thoughts rushed through his mind. "What do you mean?"

"Alyssa is married."

Maria's words ripped through Roberto's chest like the blade of a machete. His mind reeled. Married! This couldn't be! He'd thought of nothing else but Alyssa since they'd been parted. How could she? "What has happened?"

"Do you remember Diego Montalvo?"

"Diego Montalvo?   No, Maria, you can't mean it.   Not Diego!"

"You know that when Fidel took over, Alyssa's father was sent to prison.   Their house was confiscated, and her mother went crazy.   She was left with nothing but her helpless mother to care for.   Even you left her and went away to the United States.   Diego gave Alyssa and her mother a place to live.   He's close to Castro and has much power in the new government."

"I'm not surprised to hear that Diego's managed to get himself in good with Castro.   But Alyssa has married him?   I can't believe it."

"Diego was able to use his influence to have Alyssa's father moved from Matanzas Prison to a work farm.   Then he told her that, if she was his wife, Castro might be more easily persuaded to set her father free."

Roberto shook his head.   Diego.   Of all people.   "Does she love him?"

"I don't know," Maria said.   "I'm sorry for you.   I know you loved her.   Are you going to try to see her?"

Roberto turned away.   You can't have any idea how much I love her, my sister.   How could *anyone* know how much?   "No," he said, "I won't go see her.   Tell her only that I wish the best for her and her mother."

"I will," Maria said.   "I also should tell you that whenever Carlos Guave is in Havana, he comes by here.   He always asks about you and José. I think he may have been a little hurt that you didn't ask him to go with the two of you when you left. He's still in the navy and is stationed at Commando Oriente, near Guantanamo. If he knew you were here, I know he'd want to see you."

36

Roberto had come to Cuba for two reasons. One had been to see Alyssa. The other had been to recover the treasure. His first mission was a disaster. His heart was broken but there was still the treasure. The next night, he again slipped out of the safe house and made his way through the shadows across Havana. This time his destination was the Naval Academy. He observed the grounds from across the street. It appeared that nothing had changed, but he was surprised to find the academy dark and unguarded. He ran across the street and into the shadow of one of the buildings. He pressed himself against a wall and waited.

When he was satisfied that he'd been undetected, he made his way along the side of the building to its far corner. From there, he was able to get a full view of the docks. *Criollo* was at rest in her usual berth. Good. He scanned the area. He saw no movement and no lights in any of the buildings. He ran across the grass and crouched next to a locker box on the quay near *Criollo*. Still, there was no sign of anyone in the area. He moved across the concrete seawall. When he reached the boat, he stepped over the lifelines and onto the deck.

Making his way along the deck to the companionway entrance, he slid the cover back and slithered inside. He felt his way down the steps and into the blackness of the main cabin. All remained quiet. He moved to the door that led down into the engine room, unlatched it, and stepped inside.

The smell of diesel fuel filled the compartment. He closed the door behind him and switched on the flashlight he'd borrowed from Francisco. It was safe to use it now. The engine room had no portholes for light to shine through and betray his presence. He found the screwdriver Oliva used as a lever to raise the trap door leading down into the bilge. He slid the trapdoor away from the opening and shined the flashlight down into the narrow crawl space. It was clean and dry.

He squeezed himself down inside the bilge and inched along the hull on his belly until he reached another trap door above the keel. He slid this door away and directed the beam of the flashlight into the black hole beneath it. Resting on its bed of cannonball-sized rocks which the Canary Island builders had used for ballast was the old chest.

Roberto's own chest began to pound with excitement. He held the flashlight in one hand and reached down as far as he could with his other one but couldn't quite reach the chest. He slid further forward, held the flashlight between his teeth and hung by his waist.

Now, he was able to just brush the top of the chest but misjudged the distance and knocked the lid off. One corner of the old box separated and some of the jewels trickled out and down into the spaces among the rocks. Roberto pulled himself back up out of the hole. Damn!

When José and Roberto had dropped the chest into the keel the night it was given to them by Colonel Villanueva, they hadn't been concerned with its retrieval. Now with the crack opened up at one corner of the chest, even if he could reach low enough to grab it and pull it out, he would risk more jewels escaping. The box could split apart and spill its entire contents into the crevasses below. There was no choice but to go down and fill his pockets.

He dropped into the hole and scooped up handfuls of emeralds from the chest. He filled the pockets of his pants and shirt. Then he stuffed more into his socks and under his cap, until he could carry no more without the chance of losing them when he climbed out. He was leaving half of them behind, but he'd filled every empty space he had. He'd have to come back later and get the rest.

He got a grip on the ledge of the opening and pulled himself up while jewels fell from his pockets. He lay panting and perspiring in the cramped passageway of the bilge until claustrophobia began to flood over him and he clawed his way back to the engine room. There, he sat with his back against the bulkhead and tried to catch his breath, but realized he was inhaling diesel fumes, not oxygen.

Dizzy and nauseous from the foul air, Roberto stumbled to the door and pushed out of the engine room. The air was better, but he was ravenous for the fresh air up on deck. He hurried down the hall and was halfway across the main cabin before a beam of light struck him in the face.

"Who are you and what are you doing here? Answer me or I'll shoot!"

"Don't shoot, Oliva. It's me – Roberto!"

"Roberto! Jesus Christ, you scared the shit out of me!"

"Help me, Oliva. I've got to get out of here. I need fresh air. Now!"

Oliva pulled him up the ladder to the deck and helped him to the cockpit. The night air was cool and tasted sweet. He lay on his back and took long deep breaths.

"For god's sake," Oliva said, "what are you doing here, Roberto? They'll shoot you if they find you."

"Is there anyone else around?" Roberto said.

"No, the students are on break, so I'm the only one here. You're safe for a while. Rest, my friend."

"I came for the treasure."

Oliva nodded. "Ah," he said. Roberto knew the *Canario* cared nothing about money or politics, so there was no need to tell him any more than that.

"How is America?" Oliva said.

"America is good. I like it there."

"And José?"

"He's doing well. I'm sure he'll be asking me about you when I get back. What shall I tell him?"

Oliva shook his head. "Things here have changed greatly," he said. "Not for the better, I'm afraid."

"Better changes may be coming," Roberto said.

"What do you mean?"

"I can't say any more than that."

"Okay," Oliva said. "I understand. Look, you'd better get going before someone discovers you here."

Roberto pulled himself up to a sitting position. "Yes," he said. "I hope it won't be too long until I see you again."

"I hope so, too," Oliva said. *"Vaya con Dios, mi amigo."*

"Adios, Oliva." Roberto stepped over the lifelines onto the dock and slipped back into the night.

37

Roberto returned to the safe house and was met at the door by Francisco. "I'm glad you made it," Francisco said. "We were starting to get worried about you. We've received a warning from our contact inside the government that this house may no longer be safe. We were afraid we might be forced to evacuate before you got back. Get your things, Roberto, we're going to take you to Guantanamo tonight."

"But my mission isn't finished," Roberto said.

"I'm sorry," Francisco said, "we have to leave. Our operation must be suspended for the next few days until we find a new location. In the meantime, we'll have no secure place for you to stay. Both you and whatever you've already accomplished will be lost if you're discovered. And if you're caught, you become a liability to us."

Half the emeralds would be a boost to the invasion effort. Getting caught would help no one and for Roberto to jeopardize Francisco's organization would be unforgivable. "Alright," he said, "give me a minute to get ready."

He had only what he was wearing and a small canvas bag he'd left in the bedroom. Alone in the bedroom, Roberto emptied his pockets into the bag. He trusted Francisco and his team with his life, but the fewer people who knew about his mission and the emeralds, the better it would be for all concerned. Half of the jewels were still on *Criollo*. Someday, he'd be back.

"We're taking you to Parque Central," Francisco said. "There, you'll wait in the bushes near the street until your contact comes to pick you up. The contact will take you to Santiago de Cuba. From there you can get to Guantanamo."

"Good," Roberto said. "You guys work fast."

"It just happened to turn out that way," Francisco said. "You're lucky. Your contact was planning to go to the eastern end of the island, anyway."

They left the house when darkness fell. "The car will stop in front of your hiding place. The contact will be wearing a straw hat and will light a cigarette if everything appears to be safe. That's your signal to walk quickly to the car and get into the back seat. Lie down and don't say anything."

"*Muchas gracias*," Roberto said. "*Adios, amigo*. I won't forget you."

The well-trimmed Ficus hedge that lined the edge of the park was eight feet high. Roberto backed himself into it and stood motionless. Several cars passed his hiding spot and each time he prepared to walk out of the bushes and into the back seat, but none stopped. Time passed. Maybe something had gone wrong. Another car was coming. It slowed and pulled to the curb in front of him. The driver wore a wide-brimmed straw hat. Roberto waited. He saw the brim of the hat tilt forward as the driver struck a match and lit a cigarette. Roberto crossed the sidewalk and opened the passenger door. He slid into the backseat, closed the door behind him and lay down flat. Without a word, the driver put the car into gear and pulled away.

In minutes, they were on the outskirts of Havana. They headed east on Carretera Central, the highway connecting Havana with the far end of the island. Traffic thinned. A little while longer and they were the only car on the road. The driver stopped and motioned Roberto to move up to the front seat. It would be a long ride, more than 1000 kilometers. Conversation would make the trip go faster. Roberto pushed the front seat forward and opened the door. He stepped out to the shoulder of the road and stretched before getting back inside the car. Strange. What was it about this vehicle that seemed familiar? He took another step back and surveyed its silhouette. That was it. It was a Pontiac convertible like Enrique's. He slid into the front seat and exchanged glances with the driver. Her long hair was pushed up under her hat to give the impression that she was a man. Her expression of disbelief mirrored his.

"Roberto!" she said. "Roberto, my love! My God, am I dreaming? *You're* my passenger? Am I going crazy or are you really here?"

His feelings of anger and betrayal evaporated. She dove into his arms. They embraced and kissed, seeking to fill the emptiness of their time away from each other.

They separated and each searched the eyes of the other for the love that had been there the last time they were together. Alyssa turned back to the wheel. She drove until they reached a deserted side-road and turned onto it. A short distance later, she pulled off the road and parked beneath some trees. They put the top down and made love without thought of anything but each other.

They moved to the back seat and made love again. When they exhausted their passion, they lay entwined with Alyssa's head on Roberto's chest. A cool breeze blew up the hillside from the sea below. Roberto watched clouds moving in front of stars. The smell of her filled his nostrils.

She snuggled and pressed the length of her body against his. Her fingers caressed his shoulder and she thought of what to say. She wanted to tell him everything, but where to begin?

Roberto spoke first. "We waited for you at the dock as long as we could," he said.

"I'm sorry, Roberto. We were on our way to meet you when we ran into Diego. He stopped us as we were leaving my father's jail cell. *Papi* had told me we should go with you to the U.S., but

Diego made the guards take us to a room. He insisted we sit and talk with him. I kept trying to get away, but I couldn't without risking that all of you would be caught. Diego kept talking. I wanted to smash his face and make him shut up. I knew you'd have to leave without us. My heart was breaking, knowing I'd never see you or José again, but there was nothing I could do. It was awful, Roberto."

She'd sacrificed herself so they could get away. He pulled her tight against him.

There was more she had to tell him. "Roberto…," she hesitated and searched for the courage to say what must be said, "…I had to marry Diego."

"I know, Alyssa. Maria told me. It's alright."

"I'm so sorry, Roberto. I had to. Do you understand me? I had to. I've still never let him touch me. The thought of those long boney fingers moving across my body makes me ill."

A wave of compassion washed over Roberto for all that Alyssa was going through and the sacrifices she was making. He squeezed her tighter.

"He said he'd get my father out of prison. What could I do?"

Roberto stroked her hair. "I know. It's alright. I'm the one who's sorry. It's my fault, Alyssa. I wasn't here to help you."

"It's *not* your fault! It's the way things are, that's all. Castro's a pig!"

"Is your father free?"

"No, but he's been moved from Matanzas Prison to Las Canteras de Miranda. It's a prison work farm at the other end of the island, near Santiago de Cuba. I'm going there to visit him now. Diego tells me he's trying to get him out, but I don't think he's trying very hard. He's Castro's personal attorney and one of his closest advisers. If he really wanted to get my father out, he would have done it by now. I think he's just manipulating me."

"And how's your mother?"

"Not well. Her heart and her mind are both broken. I think she's given up. She's very weak and every day she gets worse. I don't think she'll live much longer."

"I'm so sorry."

Alyssa sat up and looked at him. She'd forgotten how unexpected it was for him to be there. "What are you doing here, Roberto?"

"There are secret plans to invade Cuba and take it back from Castro. I'm here to help make preparations."

"Those plans are not as secret as you think," Alyssa said. "Even I know about the invasion."

"You *know* about it? How?"

"Castro knows about it, too. It's not being kept very quiet, Roberto. Diego tells me almost everything that's going on. What he doesn't tell me, I get from going through the papers on his desk. Then I give all the information to Francisco and the underground. There aren't many secrets around here these days."

"You're Francisco's informant inside the government?"

She gave him a mischievous smile. "*Sí*, it's me," she said.

"That's very dangerous, Alyssa. If you're caught, they can shoot you as a spy."

"I'm careful. I must do it. It's the only revenge I can get against them. It's all I have. And your family, Roberto. Is everyone alright?"

"My mother died the night we left. It was a mistake to make her go. Her heart was broken. She missed Maria so much that she jumped overboard to come back here and drowned. We looked for her for a long time, but we couldn't find her. I didn't tell Maria."

"Oh, Roberto, that's too terrible. I'm so sorry. And your father, is he okay?"

"It was very hard for him, but I think he's going to be alright. He has a job rolling cigars in Miami."

"And José and Uncle Enrique, how are they?"

"They're fine. José and I are working for the CIA to prepare for the invasion. They won't tell us that it's the CIA, but we know that it must be. And Enrique's happy. He has all the cars he ever wants to fix."

"I miss José so much."

"He misses you, too. He said to give you a big kiss when I saw you."

"You did."

"Yes, but those were for me."

38

The prison work farm of Las Canteras de Miranda was better than Matanzas prison only in that he was able to go outside. The food was just as bad and there was never enough of it. Villanueva tried to supplement his prison rations with fruit that he found on the trees or picked up from the ground at the plantations where he was sent to work. Many of the farms were near the water and sometimes he could find a coconut that had washed up on the beach. Lately, however, they'd had him working in a coffee bean field and there was nothing to eat.

Each morning, he was left alone at the coffee bean field. Soon after he was dropped off, a truck would deliver a large mound of fertilizer for him to spread around the trees. Each day, he felt himself starving a little more. The morning came when he no longer had the energy to spread the fertilizer. He knew if he tried, he'd die, but he had to do something with it. He'd be beaten if the guards found anything left of the pile. That's when he began to conserve what remained of his energy by digging one big hole and burying the fertilizer in it. It was a matter of survival. Then he'd lie inert in the shade of a tree, until the truck came back to pick him up.

Villanueva had dug his hole for the day and was resting when a little, black boy came walking up the dusty road. The boy's clothes were rags, and he had no shoes. He was selling cookies his mother had made and had two left. He saw Villanueva lying beneath the tree and stopped. "Are you alright, *señor*?" he said.

"I'm very hungry," Villanueva said.

The boy looked at his two remaining cookies and then at Villanueva. "I have some cookies if you'd like to buy one," he said.

"I'd like one of your cookies very much, but I don't have any money."

The boy walked to where Villanueva was lying and gave him one of his cookies.

"I can't take it," Villanueva said. "I can't pay you."

"I know," the boy said. "I'm giving it to you."

"But won't you get in trouble with your mother when you get home? She'll expect you to have money for the cookies you've sold."

The boy shrugged. "I'll tell her *I* ate it."

"Thank you," Villanueva said. He ate only a little at a time and chewed each bite slowly. "It's the best cookie I've ever had."

The boy watched while he ate. Villanueva finished eating the cookie and thanked the boy again. "What's your name, *hijo*?"

"Cristobal," the boy said.

"You've given me the best present I've ever received, Cristobal," Villanueva said. "You're a fine boy."

Alyssa was furious when she arrived at Las Canteras de Miranda and saw the condition her father was in. The prison supervisor had been alerted that she was coming. He held Villanueva back from going out to the farms that day and gave him an extra ration of food. Her father's thin and feeble appearance sparked Alyssa to unleash a scathing tirade upon the administrator.

"He gets the same as everybody else," the administrator said and walked away.

"Do you feel alright, father?" Alyssa said.

"I'm always hungry. How's Juliana?"

"She's no better."

"And how are *you*, my dear daughter?"

"I'm fine, Papi. I've had to marry Diego." She saw the pain in his eyes at her marriage to the man who'd arrested him and taken him to jail. "It's alright," she said. "He's caring for us." She looked around to make sure no one could overhear her. "Roberto's outside hiding in the car."

"He's here? Why? I thought he went to the U.S."

"He and José are working with the CIA to free Cuba from Castro."

"Good." Villanueva guessed Roberto must have come back for the emeralds, but he didn't want to tell Alyssa this for the same reason that he himself didn't want to know where Roberto and José had hidden them. If anyone suspected that Alyssa knew about the treasure, she might be tortured to divulge its location. If Diego ever found out about it, it would be very bad for her.

"I'll talk with Diego about getting you more food," Alyssa said.

"Thank you, my daughter. Say hello to Roberto and give your mother a big hug for me. I miss you both so much."

Alyssa held back her tears. "I will, *Papi*. We miss you too. It's just so terrible for you to be treated like this. After the invasion, we'll all be together again."

"Yes," Villanueva said, "that will be a great day. Before you go I have just one favor to ask of you." He told her the story of the poor boy and the cookie. "I think the boy saved my life that day. His name was Cristobal."

Alyssa understood his reason for telling the story and placed her hand on his. "Yes, Papi," she said. "If Roberto and I have a son one day, I promise to name him after the boy."

"Okay," Alyssa said to the lump under the blanket when she returned to the car. "Now I'll take you to the safe house at Santiago de Cuba."

"How's the colonel?"

"They're starving him to death. Diego will hear about it."

Darkness had fallen by the time they arrived at the safe house. The contact led them to a windowless bedroom at the rear of the house. "Do you know Carlos Guave?" Roberto asked the contact. "He's a naval officer at Commando Oriente."

"Captain Guave? *Sí*, I know who he is," said the contact.

"Could you get a message to him and let him know I'm here?"

"*Sí*, I think I can do that, but you'll have to meet him somewhere else. The location of the safe house must be kept secret."

"I understand," Roberto said.

"Carlos, the one who couldn't defecate?" Alyssa said when the contact had gone.

Roberto smiled. "Yes, the same."

Alyssa put her arms around him. "I have to leave in the morning," she said. "Diego will be wondering what's taking me so long. But we have tonight, *mi amor.*"

"I'll have to leave soon, too," Roberto said. "I'm hoping Carlos will be able to tell me the best way to get into the U.S. Naval Base. But my heart is already missing you. I don't want to leave you, again."

"You'll be back soon, Roberto, and then we can be together always." Alyssa reached past him and flicked off the light. "Come

now and make me so happy that it will last me until you return."
She fell backwards onto the bed and pulled him down on top of her.

When Roberto awoke in the morning, she was gone. There was only her scent and a note on the pillow next to him. *"I wanted to remember our night together and not another painful goodbye. All my love, Alyssa."*

39

The sounds of his stirring brought a knock to his door. It was his contact. "Captain Guave said he'd meet you at El Toro at noon today. It's a little bar that is not far from here. You can easily walk to it in about ten minutes."

"*Gracias, amigo*," Roberto said.

A few minutes before noon, Roberto put on his baseball cap and pulled its brim down over his eyes. He wasn't likely to be recognized in this town, but he was going out in broad daylight and couldn't be too careful. The stakes were high. Discovery would mean death.

Carlos was already in the bar when Roberto arrived. He was sitting in a dark booth in the corner. The bar was empty but for Carlos and the bartender. Carlos looked different and it took Roberto a moment to realize that he was wearing glasses. Carlos rose when Roberto approached, and they embraced.

"I've missed you, *amigo*," Carlos said. Thank you for contacting me. I know it's very dangerous for you." He stopped talking when the bartender approached. "*Dos Polars, por favor,*"

Carlos said to the man. The bartender brought the beers to their table and returned to his place behind the bar.

"I see you now wear glasses," Roberto said. "You're beginning to age, my friend."

Carlos laughed. "I tell you, Roberto, I'd be lost without them. I think my eyes have always been bad, but I just never knew it. When I got the glasses, the whole world seemed to come into focus."

"Carlos," Roberto said, "I need your help to leave the country again. I want to get onto the U.S. Naval base. If I can get there, they'll send a plane to take me back to the U.S."

"I'll help you," Carlos said. "But you must let me go with you, *amigo*."

Roberto sat back. He hadn't counted on this. Cuba was even more repressive now than when they'd left in his father's boat. Regular patrols had been established at all likely escape venues. Getting out now would be dangerous enough for one man. Two men trying to leave together would be doubly difficult. "You want to leave Cuba, Carlos? Why?"

"I'm a religious man," Carlos said. "I want to go to church. But I'm also a military man. It's required that a military man always be in uniform. But it's a crime for a military man to be in church with his uniform on. So, what can I do? If I go to church out of uniform, I'll be arrested for not wearing my uniform. If I go into the church with my uniform on, I'll be arrested for wearing my uniform in the church. I thought Castro would be a great leader, but the country is crazy now. I can't live like this anymore. Please, Roberto, I must go with you. I want to be able to worship God in a church. I'm lost here, *amigo*."

Roberto ran a finger through the condensation on the side of his beer bottle. How could he refuse? "Okay, Carlos," he said. "You can come. Now tell me, are you familiar with the United States naval base at Guantanamo?"

"*Sí*! I know it very well. *Gracias*, Roberto, *gracias*." Carlos clasped his hands together and shook them in a gesture of having had a prayer answered. "We can't go by land. It's too dangerous. There are mines and barbed wire and many patrols. They catch people all the time. I think it best to go by water, although there are patrols in the channel, too. We'll have to go at night."

"Where can we get a boat?"

"We can't get a boat," Carlos said. "The only people who have boats besides the patrols are spies and fishermen who Castro trusts."

"Can we borrow one from somebody? They'll get it back."

"It would be very suspicious for us to even ask anyone. We must try another way. How about air mattresses? I think I know where I can get a couple. Those little rubber ones, like children use at the beach."

"That could work," Roberto said. "It doesn't seem like we have much choice. Where could we get into the water without being detected?"

"It would have to be up in the bay somewhere, away from the channel where the patrol boats are. There's a salt processing plant in Glorieta. Next to the plant is a ditch that runs from the road down to Caimamera Bay, which connects to Guantanamo Bay. I think we could get into the water there without being seen."

"How far is Glorieta from the naval base?"

"A long way," Carlos said. "Probably about twenty kilometers."

"That is a long way," Roberto said. "If we leave at high tide, it'll help us float down the bay to the channel as it goes out. We'll need to go on a night when there's a high tide and no moon."

"I'll look at the charts," Carlos said.

"Can you get me a bathing suit and a pair of swimming fins?"

"I'll try."

"Get some petroleum jelly, too. It'll protect us from sharks. Also, see if you can get a length of line and a diving knife with a sheath that I can tie around my leg. We may need it."

It was two days before Roberto heard from Carlos. His message said he'd secured two brown air mattresses and the other things Roberto wanted. He'd also found a friend in the forestry department who would drive them to Glorieta. They'd ride beneath a tarp in the back of a truck and jump out when they reached the ditch next to the salt processing plant. The ditch ran down to the bay. Their signal to jump would be when the man slapped his hand twice against the side of the truck, but the driver would only slow down, not stop. Roberto was to meet Carlos at El Toro bar in three days, just after dark. From El Toro, they'd go to a dirt road on the outskirts of town where the truck would pick them up to take them to Glorieta. There'd be no moon that night and an outgoing tide would float them down the bay.

When Roberto arrived at El Toro, Carlos was sitting in a booth. He had a small canvas bag. Roberto had his own canvas bag…the one that contained the emeralds. It was cinched at the top with a drawstring. "Do you have everything?" he asked Carlos.

"Yes," Carlos said. "High tide's at ten o'clock. What do you have in *your* bag?"

Roberto shook his head. "I'm sorry, Carlos. I can't tell you what's in it, but it's important. It's my mission to get this bag to the United States. If anything happens to me, it'll be up to you to get it to José."

"How would I find him?"

"Get to Guantanamo and say you need to see Chip Magner. Someone there will know how to reach him. And Magner will know where José is."

"You mean that big, red-headed guy on *Finnisterre*?"

"Yes. Now, no more questions. The less you know, the better. Okay, *amigo*?"

"Okay," Carlos said. "We'd better get going."

When they reached the dirt road, they walked down it a short distance before moving into the woods to wait. Soon they heard the rattling approach of the forestry truck. They stepped out from their hiding place and the truck stopped. They jumped into the back of the truck and covered themselves with the tarp. Their hearts were pounding like jackhammers, but so far, the plan was working.

It was probably only one hour, but it seemed like several before they heard the man's hand slap twice against the side of the truck. Roberto leaped out first and was followed by Carlos. They hit the ground running and headed for the drainage ditch. The ditch was dry and deep, but they still had to crouch low as they ran to stay out of sight. The area looked deserted, but they were taking no chances.

When they reached the water, they stripped off their clothes, got into their bathing suits and smeared themselves with petroleum jelly. Carlos gave Roberto the sheath with the knife and the length of line he'd asked for. Roberto cut off ten meters of the line and wrapped it around his waist. He put several loops through a strap on his canvas bag. His plan was to lie on his back and paddle. This way, he could carry the bag on his stomach. He tied the sheath and knife to his leg. Then they blew up the air mattresses. They put their clothes in Carlos's bag, loaded it with rocks and threw it far out into the bay. The water felt warm when Roberto waded into it.

Carlos stepped in and looked around him in the water. "I don't like this," he said. He jumped. "A fish! I felt a fish!"

"Be quiet," Roberto said. "What's the matter?"

"I'm sorry, Roberto. It gives me the creeps being in the water at night."

"Get hold of yourself. We've got a long way to go," Roberto said.

The tide was beginning to turn when they got on their rafts and continued to grow in strength as they paddled down the shoreline. There was no moon, but enough starlight to be able to see the bottom through the clear water. Phosphorescence in the water made green streaks as their hands stroked through it. Small fish, startled when they passed over them, shot away and left their own trails of phosphorescence.

As they floated down the bay, they made their way out further from shore. Their goal was Cayo Brooks, a small island in the middle of the channel. There they would wait through the daylight hours until darkness fell again. They paddled all night. The sun was reaching the horizon, and the tide was nearly out when they finally reached Cayo Brooks. As they pushed their way in among the mangroves, they were attacked by swarms of mosquitoes and no-see-ums, the biting gnats that drive animals insane. They slipped off the rafts and dug up mud from the bottom to smear over their heads and faces to deter the insects. They kept their bodies submerged and their eyes closed. They would have to stay in water up to their necks until darkness came again.

It was near midday when Roberto heard an approaching motorboat. They'd seen the lights of patrol boats moving up and down the shoreline during the night, but this was the first to have ventured so far out into the bay. Roberto sank down. His nostrils touched the water. He opened his eyes and watched the boat coming just outside the mangroves. It wasn't a patrol boat, but a fisherman in a dory with an outboard motor.

The boat passed in front of the men and the fisherman looked over. His eyes met Roberto's. The fisherman looked away and pretended not to have seen anything, but Roberto knew there'd been a fleeting exchange of recognition. The fisherman continued to putt-putt along the shore of the island.

Only a man loyal to Castro could have a boat. If he reported what he'd seen, patrol boats would be sent to the island to look for them. If Roberto and Carlos were captured, they'd be shot. Panic flooded through Roberto. There was no choice…he must kill the fisherman. It was the only way to be sure he wouldn't alert the authorities. He ripped the knife from its sheath and jumped to his feet. Running as fast as he could through the thick mangroves, his bare feet tripped and splashed through the tangles of roots. He raced to where he could intercept the boatman when he rounded the tip of the island. Adrenaline raged through his body and his heart hammered with his exertions, his panic, and the horror of what he was about to do.

When he reached the tip of the island Roberto took a last leap and hurtled through the leaves and branches. Naked but for his bathing suit and covered in mud, he held his knife high, ready to be driven down deep into the fisherman's neck. He exploded from the mangroves and landed in the shallows at the water's edge, but the man wasn't there. The boat was bearing away from the island beyond Roberto's reach.

His blood cooled, as he watched the fisherman motor away. Part of him was relieved that he hadn't been able to kill the man, but now he and Carlos were at risk. The man would report them to the authorities and patrol boats would come. He turned and worked his way back to his hiding place next to Carlos.

They didn't hear the chugging of the patrol boat until it was almost dark. They could hear the voices of the men on the boat as they swept spotlights along the shore of the island. The boat circled Cayo Brooks several times, but the men didn't see them and left. When they were gone, Roberto punched holes in the mattresses until only the pillow section was left inflated.

Carlos's jaw fell open. "What're you doing, Roberto? Are you losing your mind? The channel from here to Guantanamo is known to be full of sharks!"

"We'll float lower in the water and have less profile. The patrol boats are looking for us and now we'll be harder to see."

"But what about the sharks? They'll be able to get us."

"They could have gotten us before. We had to do this."

Carlos shivered. "I think I'd rather be shot by *Fidelistas* than eaten by sharks."

They struck out from the mangroves with Roberto leading the way. They put the inflated pillow sections of the air mattresses under their chests and dog paddled. Roberto shifted the canvas bag to his back. They tried to not splash their arms and legs to keep from attracting the sharks. The tide was running out again, so they aimed for a spot on the shore just up from the naval base. Roberto calculated that this course would put them at the naval base when they reached land. The wind was blowing and kicked up the water into small whitecaps. The waves made it difficult to watch for patrol boats but would also make it harder for the patrols to see them.

They were halfway across when they ran into a school of jellyfish. They were big white ones, two feet across with stinging tentacles that burned like fire when they touched the bare skin of the men. Roberto had seen this type of jellyfish before and managed to avoid most of them by placing his hand on their tops and pushing them aside.

Carlos screamed. He'd been stung.

"Watch what I'm doing!" Roberto said. "It's only the tentacles dangling down below them that can sting you. It's safe to touch them on the top. Put your hand on the tops of them and push them to the side as you swim."

Roberto made it out of the jellyfish into clear water and began to swim toward the eastern shore of the channel and the lights of the U.S. Naval base. Behind him, he heard Carlos scream again. He yelled for him to be quiet, but Carlos kept screaming. Roberto turned around and swam back to help him. Carlos was flailing helplessly, crazy with pain from the stings of the jellyfish. Roberto slapped him. "Be quiet, or you'll get us both killed."

"I can't see, Roberto. My glasses are caked with salt. Help me."

Roberto unwound his line and tied one end around Carlos's armpits and the other end around his own waist. "Lie on your back, Carlos, and hold the pillow under your neck." He paddled back through the jellyfish, pushing them aside as he'd done before and towing Carlos behind him. Carlos continued to moan, but at least he was no longer screaming. "Kick your feet," Roberto called over his shoulder. "Give me some help!"

They were now only a hundred meters from shore. Roberto could see two American sentries standing on a dock, fishing. A large trail of phosphorescence flashed beneath him. Shark! And a big one. He put his head underwater, but it was too dark to see anything. The water conducted the steady chug-chug of an approaching patrol boat to his ears. That's it, he thought, we've got to get out of here.

Roberto dove beneath the surface to swim faster and keep from splashing. His energy was spent and his lungs were screaming when he saw the pilings of the dock and exploded up onto the surface. The shocked sentries helped them up to the dock, laughing at their own surprise, until they saw the skin falling away from the men's bodies where they'd been stung by the jellyfish.

<h1 style="text-align:center">40</h1>

Severely dehydrated and suffering skin lesions, nausea and cramping from the multiple jellyfish stings, Roberto and Carlos recuperated for two weeks in the Guantanamo Bay naval base infirmary. They were then flown, not back to Miami as they expected, but to Washington D.C. They landed at Anacosta Naval Air Station, across the Potomac from the capitol, where they were met by Chip Magner. On the way to the CIA offices at Quarters Eye, Magner eyed the canvas bag in Roberto's lap. "Did you get it?"

Roberto patted the bag. "I have it."

"Good."

"He's been carrying that bag with him wherever he goes," Carlos said from the back seat. "He even takes it with him to the bathroom. What's in that bag, anyway?"

"It's a long story…very long. I'll tell you all about it once we get this package to where it's going," Roberto said.

When they reached CIA headquarters at Quarters Eye, Roberto followed Magner to a private office. They sat across the desk from each other. Carlos was being debriefed in another office about Cuban military strength. "Okay, let's see what you've got," Magner said,

Roberto untied the drawstring of the canvas bag, turned it upside down and spilled its contents onto the desk. Magner sat spellbound watching the jewels stream from the bag. "They're real?"

"They're real," Roberto said.

"They must be worth millions." Magner couldn't take his eyes from the glittering green mound.

"Probably," Roberto said.

"I had no idea this was what you were talking about when you said there was funding for the invasion back in Cuba. Are you sure you want to do this…give all this up for the operation?"

"These emeralds belong to the people of Cuba. I can think of no better use for them than to free the Cuban people from tyranny."

"Alright," Magner said. "We'll have them appraised and get every penny we can for them. How do you want the money to be spent?"

"When I was in Cuba, I was introduced to some of the leaders of the underground. They told me that the guerillas in the mountains are starving and poorly equipped. I'd like to send them food and supplies."

"Okay, we can airdrop anything they need. Much of the invasion force is also in need of uniforms," Magner said.

"Alright," Roberto said. "The rest of the money can be spent on uniforms and weapons for the invasion force. Is José still on Useppa Island?"

"No. He's been training with the brigade in Guatemala and will be meeting us in Puerto Rico. We'll fly you and Carlos there when you've finished your debriefings here."

Roberto laughed. "*Now* what?"

"You guys used to be at the Naval Academy in Cuba. How'd you like to be frogmen?"

"*Hombres ranas?*"

"Yep, we're going to train a few men in swimming and underwater demolition techniques at Vieques Island…a little garden spot just off the Puerto Rican coast. You're gonna love it. Your mission will be to land ahead of the invasion force and place lights on the beaches to show the brigade where to come ashore."

When Roberto told Carlos about the underwater training, he shook his head. Their escape to Guantanamo was still fresh in his mind. "No thanks," he said. "I've had enough swimming for one war. I think I'll stick with the brigade."

40

Havana, Cuba

Colonel Alfredo Gomez was enjoying the good life. He was living in a confiscated house, compliments of the revolution. He received bribes from families seeking favorable treatment for relatives locked in his prisons. People stood when he walked into a room and knelt before him as they pleaded for mercy of a loved one. Minister of Prisons was a profitable position.

But the situation with Colonel Villanueva vexed him. The old man sounded like he really didn't know where the treasure was. If so, what had happened to it? Gomez began to wonder if the value of the treasure was not in the emeralds themselves, but in the information that they existed.

His reverie was interrupted by the sound of rapid footsteps in the hallway. They stopped outside his office and the door was thrown open…Diego Montalvo and he didn't look happy.

Gomez jumped to attention when Diego strode into his office. "*Señor* Montalvo, what an…"

Gomez was cut short by a dismissive gesture from Diego who lifted a chair and slammed it back to the floor before sitting. He hoisted his long feet up onto Gomez's desk and crossed his legs in ceremonial pomp. Diego completed the drama of his entrance by raising his eyes to the ceiling and exhaling in exasperation before training a withering gaze upon Gomez. "My wife went to visit her father, again. She tells me her father is starving. Why is my father-in-law starving, Colonel Gomez? Did we not discuss a similar situation regarding this man some weeks ago? Did I not make it clear he was to receive preferential treatment?"

Gomex sputtered. "Wife? You've married Villanueva's daughter? I'm sorry, s*eñor* Montalvo, I didn't know. I have a tight budget and the amount of food the prisoners get is determined by the money allotted to my depart…"

Diego slapped his hand hard on the arm of his chair. "My concern is not for your budget or the condition of the other prisoners, Colonel Gomez! My concern is only for my father-in-law. I don't want my wife to complain to me about her father's health. That's unacceptable! Am I making myself clear, Colonel Gomez?"

"*Sí*, s*eñor* Montalvo, *sí*," Gomez said. "I'll arrange for the prisoner Villanueva to have extra rations, immediately!" His job wasn't easy. He'd been struggling with the inadequate funds given him to run the prison system ever since they'd given him the job.

Cuba became a very poor country when Castro nationalized the businesses and the United States responded by boycotting Cuban products. At the same time, the prison population was rising. The government identified more enemies of the state every day. He had to staff the prisons with enough guards to control the inmates and there was little left over for food. He'd already cut expenses to the bare bones. Now it had become commonplace for prisoners to starve to death. It happened daily. In fact, he'd come to rely upon these deaths as a way of reducing the prison population.

"Then that is taken care of," Diego said. "Now, if you don't feel you're qualified to continue in your current position, Colonel Gomez, please tell me. I'm sure we can find someone else to be Minister of Prisons if you're finding the job too difficult for you."

Gomez prickled under the implication of this veiled threat. If he were not careful, he might soon find *himself* in prison under some fabricated charge of misappropriation of funds or other manufactured transgression. Until now, he'd been withholding his knowledge of Villanueva's treasure from Montalvo. Perhaps it was time to play this card. It was imperative that he stay in the good graces of this man, but how to begin? He cleared his throat. "I have some, ah, information," he said, "which I think it important to share with you, *señor* Montalvo."

Diego relaxed and leaned back in his chair. "Information?" He clasped his hands behind his head. "Go ahead, Colonel Gomez, I'm always interested in information."

"I haven't said anything prior to this out of consideration for your relationship with the Villanueva family," Gomez said. He couched his words in respectful terms to keep his revealing of this secret from backfiring upon him in a fit of rage from Montalvo. Gomez had witnessed enough of this man's quick temper and wanted to risk none of its potential consequences.

"Go on," Diego said.

"I first met your wife and her mother many years ago when I commanded the garrison at Santa Fe. Your wife was just a child, then. They were vacationing at the beach, and I was fortunate to be able to rescue her from drowning. Your wife's father, Colonel Villanueva, was an important man in those days and he thanked me personally. He even arranged for me to receive official recognition for what I'd done."

"Really?" Diego said. He'd known nothing of any relationship between Gomez and the Villanuevas.

Gomez continued but included nothing about the benefits he'd received from his relationship with Villanueva. "A couple of years later, when I was on patrol, I found a man digging a big hole at the beach, near the Taoro river. I was told a fantastic tale about a buried treasure and confiscated an old map from the man. I informed him that any treasure that might be discovered belonged to the government of Cuba. I then had the area roped off and ordered an excavation of the site by steam shovel."

Diego dropped his feet from Gomez's desk to the floor. "A treasure?"

"*Sí*," Gomez said. "I doubted it as well, but I thought we should at least look, and it turned out to be true. The steam shovel uncovered an old chest. I took it to the garrison and locked it in the safe while I thought about what to do with it. I knew the government of Batista was corrupt and that the true owners of the chest, the people of Cuba, would never hear of the treasure if I reported it through channels."

Diego was leaning forward now with his elbows on Gomez's desk. He pressed his palms together. His forefingers supported his chin, and the tips of his middle fingers touched his lips. "*Sí! Sí!*" he said. "This is fantastic. So, what did you do?"

Gomez knew that he had Montalvo now. He mused for a moment how fascinating it was that riches always seemed to interest those who already had them, even more than those who didn't. "The only man of any consequence I thought I might be able to trust was Colonel Villanueva, so I took the chest to him. I was careful not to open it until we were together and could discover its contents at the same time. The chest was locked and corroded, so we broke the lock and pried the box open with a crowbar."

"*Sí! Sí!* What did you find!?"

Gomez recalled the wonder of seeing the jewels that day at Colonel Villanueva's cottage. "It was unbelievable," he said. "The chest was filled with emeralds."

"Emeralds! This *is* unbelievable. What happened to them?"

"That is what I don't know," Gomez said. "After I left them with Villanueva that day, I never heard any more about them."

"Does my wife know about this?"

"I don't know," Gomez said, "but I don't see how she could not know. She and her father are very close."

Diego leaned back in his chair, the tips of his fingers still to his lips. "Yes," he said. "She surely must know something."

42

Puerto Cabezas, Nicaragua
April 1, 1961

After their underwater training in Puerto Rico, Roberto, José, and the rest of the frogmen were taken to Nicaragua, which would be the jumping off spot for the invasion. Magner met them at the dock and gave them a reception at the "biggest and loudest bar in town."

"So, when do we go in?" Roberto asked.

"It better be damn soon," Magner said. "Our intelligence is telling us that Castro's being strengthened by the Russians. He's getting MiG-21 fighters, and his pilots will be fully trained by May. We need to get in there before that happens. Right now, his air force is fairly weak…only a few B-26's, some British Sea Furies and a couple of T-33's. Our target date to have everything operational is April 15th."

"How are we going to deal with the planes he already has?" Roberto said.

"The plan is to knock out his planes with preliminary bombing raids while they're still on the ground. That'll guarantee us air superiority and give our guys time to land and establish a beachhead.   Once that's accomplished and a provisional government's been established, we expect the *revolutionarios* in the mountains to join us. Then the populace will rise up and take their country back."

José nodded. "That's it," he said. "All the people really need is the belief that they can actually win."

"How much support can we expect from the Americans?" Roberto said.

"Well, air support, certainly, if necessary," Magner said. "And there will be a naval presence. But keep in mind that this is supposed to look like an all-Cuban operation. The U.S. doesn't want to risk giving the Russians an edge in world opinion by looking like they're picking on Castro. And they don't want to give Kruschev an excuse to take Berlin. American forces would only become engaged in an absolute necessity."

"What if we get stalled on the beaches?" José said.

"That's a good question," Magner said. "We need to be prepared for any eventuality. One reason we've chosen this landing site is because it's near the Escambray Mountains. If the invasion fails, the brigade can slip into the Escambrays and join the rebels."

"When does the brigade get here?" José said.

"Starts tomorrow. They figure it's going to take them three days to get everybody over here from Guatemala."

"How many are there now?" Roberto said.

"Last I heard, almost 1500."

José looked around the bar. "We've gotta bring Carlos here. This is his kind of place."

"Well, you're going to have to swim in," Magner said. "After tonight, this place will be off limits."

"No problem," José said. "We're frogmen.

Ross, who would be Magner's partner for the operation, flew in from Washington with bad news. He'd been in meetings with CIA brass at Quarters Eye. He spread out the maps and charts. "There's been a change in plans," he said.

"Change? What change?" Magner said.

"There's been a change in the landing zone. We'll be going in at Bahia de Cochinos instead of Trinidad."

Magner exploded. "You've got to be kidding! Why the change? Goddamit, the plan we agreed on was to land at Trinidad. This is fuckin' stupid. For starters, Bahia de Cochinos is too far from the Escambrays for the mountains to be used as a fallback position if things go badly. There's not even a dock. Whose bright idea was this, anyway?"

"Take it easy, Chip. Personally, I happen to agree with you, but plans change. There's a big push up in Washington to keep this whole thing as quiet as possible and the Joint Chiefs decided Bahia de Cochinos would draw less attention."

Magner was incredulous. "They want to keep it quiet? Good luck. It's an invasion…invasions aren't quiet, Ross. This is unbelievable. Do you know what Bahia de Cochinos means in English? Do you? Bay of Pigs, for crissake! And that's exactly what it's going to be if we go in there."

"Look," Ross said, "with the way the mood is in Washington, we're lucky to be going in anywhere. I think if we weren't so far along with this operation that they'd scrap the whole thing. I'm supposed to get back to them today with a final report on our preparedness. So, what's it gonna be? Are we ready, or not?"

"Damn right we're ready. These guys are so fired up that if Washington were to pull the plug on this operation, I think the brigade would go anyway…even if they had to swim all the way there. The only way to stop them would be to shoot them all right here in Nicaragua or sink the troop ships on the way there.

"Good, that's what I wanted to hear."

The brigade ships left Puerto Cabezas just after midnight on April 14. The frogmen had been assigned to the *Blagar,* which would serve as their command ship. Magner called the frogmen into the briefing room and put up a chart. "We're going to rendezvous with the other ships here, eighteen miles southeast of Cayo Largo. Our landing point is another nine miles, here at Playa Giron, which has been designated Blue Beach."

Roberto was seeing the map of the Bahia de Cochinos area for the first time. He'd never been to the area when he lived in Cuba and knew it only as the location of the Zapata Swamp. The bay was long and narrow. It looked as though God had pressed his thumb down on the land and left a long deep imprint, which had then filled with water. On the right side of the entrance to the bay was Playa Giron and Blue Beach.

"We'll go in first and place lights to mark the landing area," Magner said. "The 4th and 6th Battalions will land there at fifteen minutes after midnight on the 17th and secure the airfield. Eighteen miles further inland, up here at the head of Bahia de Cochinos is Playa Larga, which has been designated as Red Beach. Ross and his men will land there at 3:00 A.M., followed by the 2nd and 5th Battalions. Over here, five miles east of Blue Beach is Green Beach, where we'll land the 3rd Battalion at 6:30."

Roberto studied the topography of the charts. Other than the beaches themselves, everything else was swamp. Two narrow roads had been carved through the swamps from the mainland, one into Playa Larga and one into Playa Giron. There was also a beach road, which ran along the bay, connecting Playa Larga and Playa Giron.

"The 1st Battalion paratroopers will jump at first light," Magner said. "One company here, just north of Red Beach and the rest of them up here about eight miles inland of Playa Giron at San Blas. Any questions? None? Then, *vaya con Dios*, men."

44

Havana

April 15

The morning after his conversation with Gomez, Diego confronted Alyssa at breakfast. "So, tell me what you know about the treasure."

"Treasure? What are you talking about? What treasure?"

Diego retold the story Gomez had related to him. "This is official business I'm asking you about, Alyssa, and very important. You must know something about this."

"I'm telling you, Diego, there's nothing for me to know. This story is too fantastic to be believed. There can't be any treasure. If the story was true, of course I would've known about it. I do remember Sergeant Gomez coming to our house in Santa Fe once, but it was only to see my mother."

"*Sergeant* Gomez? But this man is an officer." Diego began to put the pieces together. Villanueva must have arranged for Gomez to become an officer in exchange for his silence about the treasure. "Since you refuse to tell me anything, then I'll go and speak to your father, myself."

"No, Diego! Leave my poor father alone…please. He knows nothing about this crazy tale which has been fabricated by Gomez, surely for his own reasons! Don't be stupid, Diego."

"I'm going to see your father. While I'm gone, you will not leave this house."

"Not leave the house? What do you mean?"

"Exactly that. Until I solve the mystery of the treasure's whereabouts, I cannot trust you to leave the house. If you will not help me, then you must be confined until I sort this out.

"This is insane!" Alyssa said. "There's no treasure. This man has made it all up. Can't you see?"

"One last time, Alyssa," Diego said. "Will you help me or not?"

"I can't help a crazy man!"

Diego rose from his chair and threw his napkin on the table. "If you won't help me, I won't be responsible for the consequences," he said.

"I *cannot* help you, Diego, because there is no treasure. And the way you're acting, even if there was a treasure, I most certainly would not help you."

Diego turned his back to her and strode toward the door. Alyssa's pent-up frustration and anger surged to the surface. No longer able to hide her true feelings, they erupted out of her. "You're a horrible man, Diego! You're disgusting and I hate you! I've always hated you!"

These parting words stung Diego like a lash. He slammed and locked the door behind him. After all he'd done for her. And the risks he'd taken for her father. Well, that was all over. She'd only been using him. He would be the fool no longer.

A government plane had been assigned for his use. Diego took it to the east end of the island. He was still burning from Alyssa's rebuke when he walked into the headquarters at Las Canteras de Miranda farm prison. "Bring me the prisoner, Villanueva!"

The old man was brought before him in shackles, but there was something about Villanueva's presence that caused Diego to stand when he entered the room. "I am Diego Montalvo," he said. "Please be seated, *señor*."

Villanueva sat in a chair across the table from Diego and said nothing. He recognized this man as his son-in-law but was willing to give no recognition to the fact. He regarded Diego as one of Castro's parasites, crawling inside the fallen fruit that was once Cuba.

"I know about the treasure," Diego said. "Tell me where it is."

Villanueva stared back at Diego without response.

"If you don't tell me, I will have you tortured," Diego said. "I'm tired of playing games with your family."

Villanueva remained silent.

"If after having you tortured, you still do not tell me, I will have your wife and daughter imprisoned as collaborators. They, too, will be tortured until I get the information that I want."

"You would torture your own wife? You're lower than I thought."

"Recovering this treasure is a matter of State importance," Diego said.

"The State is more important to you than your family?"

Diego slammed his hand on the table. "The State *is* my family and you and my wife are betraying it."

Villanueva shook his head. "The State is an institution, created by the people for their mutual welfare. It exists to serve the people, not the other way around, as you and Castro seem to believe."

"Enough! I'm tired of this. Are you going to tell me or not?"

"I don't know where the treasure is," Villanueva said.

"Aha, then you admit there's a treasure."

"Of course, there's a treasure, but I don't know where it is. My wife and daughter know nothing of the treasure. I only know that you'll never get your hands on it."

"We'll see about that," Diego said. "Guards! Take this man to his cell and give him no more food." Diego shoved back from the table and pointed a finger at Villanueva. "I'll be back, old man. You can count on that. And when I return, you'll tell me where the treasure's hidden whether you want to or not."

When Diego returned to Havana, he had his men search the Villanueva house again. That had to be where the colonel had hidden the treasure chest after getting it from Gomez. Villanueva would have wanted to keep it close to him. Even if his men didn't find the treasure in the house, maybe they would find evidence that Villanueva once had possession of it. If Diego could prove that Villanueva had had the treasure in his house, but hadn't shared its existence with the government, he would have what he needed to threaten the old man with more charges.

Diego was there when they moved the desk in Colonel Villanueva's study. He saw the plate in the floor when the rug was pulled away. He knelt and looked down into the hole when the metal plate was removed. It was the perfect place to hide a small treasure chest. Obviously, something had been hidden there. It had to have been the emeralds.

The sun was setting when Diego flew back to Las Canteras de Miranda farm prison armed with his new information about the secret hole in Villanueva's study.   "Take me to the prisoner, Villanueva!"

They hurried toward Villanueva's cell. Diego's heart raced with the excitement and anticipation of ending this mystery and finding out where the jewels were now being hidden. Villanueva had verified that Gomez's fantastic story about a treasure was true. Diego had found the hiding place where it had been kept in Villanueva's house. Even if Villanueva was telling the truth when he insisted he didn't know where the treasure was, he surely knew who did. He must have given it to someone to take to a new hiding place when he saw that his arrest was imminent. He would have known that his house would be searched.

Diego's anger with Alyssa had not abated. For her to deny him like she had, after all he'd done for her and her family, was unforgivable. There would be no more compassion. If the old man refused to talk, Diego would have the guards do whatever was necessary to make him talk. The time for kindness was past.

They reached the wing of the farm prison, which held Villanueva's cell. "I'll first talk to him, alone," he told the guard. "Wait here at the end of the hall. I'll call you if I need you."

Diego slowed his pace. He would impress upon Villanueva that he meant business. When he reached the cell, he stamped his left heel extra hard, made a ninety-degree military pivot and trained his eyes upon the prisoner.

A chill ran through Diego's body. The old man stared back at him with empty eyes. His head leaned oddly to one side and a thin cord cut into the flesh of his neck. He hung motionless from a grate in the ceiling where the other end of the cord was tied.

After it was dark, Alyssa went in to wake her mother. They'd been trapped in the house all day. The windows on the first floor were laced with decorative iron bars to keep intruders out, but now they served to keep her in. There was no longer any sense staying in the house. Their days of protection under Diego were over. His tirade before he left made it apparent that he viewed them as the enemy. Things would only get worse. They'd have to take their chance while they had it. If they tied some bed sheets together, they could lower themselves from the railing of the second-floor balcony. Juliana had wasted away to the point that her weight would not be difficult for Alyssa to carry on her back. The only question was whether her mother would have the strength to hold on to her as Alyssa shinnied down the rope of sheets. They'd go to Francisco. He'd find a place to hide them.

Juliana was asleep when Alyssa entered her bedroom. She looked more beautiful than she had since the tragedy began and her husband had been taken from her. The lines of worry had left her face. She didn't stir when Alyssa touched her cheek, nor when she shook her shoulder. Juliana was gone.

45

The house was dark when Diego entered. Alyssa would be angry for having been locked in. He'd decided to tell her that Villanueva had died of natural causes. He called her name, but there was no response. He called again and still no answer. Where was she?

He rushed up the stairs two at a time, flicking light switches as he ran. The door to her bedroom was open, but she wasn't there. The bed was still made up. He searched the rooms upstairs, but they were empty. He ran back downstairs and into Juliana's room. She was there, asleep. Diego relaxed. Alyssa wouldn't abandon her mother and must be somewhere nearby. He went in to shake Juliana awake and was startled…her skin was cold. He shrank back in the realization that she was dead.

Diego checked the remaining downstairs rooms. "You can come out now," he called. "I won't hurt you, Alyssa. I'm sorry I was so foolish." He went back up to the second floor and again checked each of the rooms. He opened the doors to the second story veranda where he spied the evidence of Alyssa's departure. Still tied to the railing was the first of several bed sheets, which stretched to the ground. Alyssa had escaped.

Alyssa's plan was to get to Francisco. He could hide her from Diego. She hailed a cab and had it drop her a few blocks from the new safe house. She made the rest of the way on foot. She told Francisco the story of Diego's angry threats, of his locking her in the house and her mother's death. "There was no need for me to stay," she said to Francisco.

"No," Francisco agreed. "Diego Montalvo is a dangerous man. You were wise to get out of there. The invasion has begun. We're getting reports that there've been bombings at many of the airfields. The Americans will be here soon."

Alyssa sank into a chair. "Finally! Thank, God. I'll be able to free my father."

"In the meantime," Francisco said, "I think it best that you stay here. Moving around will only expose you and increase your chances of being found."

"Thank you, Francisco. You're a good and brave man. Where can I sleep? I am suddenly very tired."

Francisco showed her to a back bedroom. Alyssa collapsed on the bed fully clothed and fell immediately asleep. Francisco closed the door and returned to his radio. He'd been waiting for reports of the invasion. It wasn't long after midnight when the commentator broke in with a report of fighting near the southeastern tip of the island. The invasion was on. The work he'd done and the risks he'd taken over the past two years were finally going to result in Castro's defeat. He listened for a while as the reports of battle continued to come in. He felt like celebrating.

He opened a bottle of *rioja* and filled a small glass. He made a silent toast to Cuba and her liberators and drained the glass in one quick motion. He poured himself another and put the bottle on the table beside his chair. He rested his head against the back of the chair and smiled. Tension lifted from his body; the black days of Castro's rule would soon be over. He was beginning to drift into a delicious doze when the front door was kicked open and the room was filled with shouting armed men. Before Francisco could rise from his chair, the butt of a rifle was slammed against the side of his jaw. He was dragged from the house into the street and thrown against a wall.

"You're being executed for espionage against your country. Death to all spies and subversives!" Three men raised their rifles, and three bullets were fired into Francisco. He crumpled to the pavement.

In the back bedroom, Alyssa awoke from the sound of the front door being broken open. She heard chaos erupting from the front of the house and rolled off the bed. She slid beneath it, just as the bedroom door was thrown open and a light turned on. She could see the dusty boots of a man standing in the doorway. She held her breath and the man walked down the hall to check the other rooms.

Then she heard men dragging Francisco into the street. There was more shouting, and the sound of rifles being fired. She heard the men laughing and joking as they left. Then a truck started up and drove away.

Alyssa heard people gathering in the street to view the dead body of Francisco. Someone would be likely to come inside the house. She crawled from beneath the bed and climbed out the window. Moving around toward the front of the house, she peered around a corner. Francisco's body lay in a pool of blood surrounded by curious onlookers. She was perspiring but felt cold. A tight band of pain gripped her forehead and her stomach heaved once and then heaved again and emptied its contents next to the wall of the house. She held back a sob and said a silent prayer for her friend and protector. Then, dizzy with nausea and fear, she stumbled away through the darkness.

46

Bahia de Cochinos
April 19

After landing with the frogmen in the raft and setting the landing lights, Roberto and José moved up with the 6th Brigade and were assigned to an 81-millimeter mortar. They fired the mortar at Castro's approaching infantry until it began to melt, so they took over the mortar next to them. The soldier who'd been firing it had been killed. Something struck José's arm and knocked him down. He got up and continued to fire the mortar with his good arm. Finally, Castro's forces pulled back.

Roberto looked at José's arm. "You need medical attention, Amigo.".

"I'm okay," José said, "but things aren't looking so good here, Roberto. Where's the damn air cover? We're getting slaughtered."

"I don't know, it looks like the promises we got from the U.S. were empty ones. Just like our rifles, now."

"One of us needs to find Alyssa," José said. "Anyone who's been working with the underground is going to be in great danger. Castro will be arresting everybody."

Roberto nodded. "You're right. One of us needs to go to her."

José followed Roberto's eyes down to his mangled left arm. "Looks like it's going to have to be you, my friend," he said. "You can see that I'm right. Put a tourniquet around my arm, up by the shoulder…that'll stop the bleeding. Then, get going. There's no time to lose. Take the raft."

Roberto didn't like leaving José on the battlefield with one bad arm, but Alyssa would be in serious trouble. Getting to Havana wouldn't be easy, even with two good arms.

It seemed like it took forever to motor the raft across the mouth of Cochinos Bay. Roberto looked back through the smoke-filled haze hanging over the water. The explosions continued back on shore but were muted from this distance. Tall columns of black smoke rose from the scenes of fighting. The stench of battle still permeated his nose and lungs. Both the landscape and the events of the past few days seemed surreal. He aimed the raft toward the clear air outside the bay and inhaled its sweet freshness when it hit him, cleansing his nostrils and body of the past seventy-rwo hours, and helping to clear his mind of the bitterness of betrayal and defeat.

He passed the western edge of the bay and began to head further out from shore. From high above him came the high-pitched whine of a diving Sea Fury. Seconds later, the raft was engulfed in a hail of bullets that whizzed past him into the water. The bullets left trails of bubbles where they ripped through the shallow sea and kicked up clouds of sand as they slammed into the white seabed below.

Roberto gunned the raft toward a nearby island of mangroves. The warplane leveled off meters above his head and roared back up into the late-afternoon sky. He spied an opening among the mangroves just large enough for the raft. He could hear the fighter plane turning for another pass and powered the raft at full throttle deep into the foliage and killed the engine. He dove into the bow and curled into the smallest ball he could make of himself. Bullets sliced and crashed through the mangroves at the outer edge of the opening as the plane roared over him.

He heard the Sea Fury climbing, again. Clouds of insects swarmed around him, and he pulled a sheet of canvas up over his body. He rolled himself up in the canvas to shut them out. Huddled in the bow of the raft, he waited for the Sea Fury to dive on him, again but heard nothing more. It felt good to lie down…it had been a long time. He ached to get to Alyssa but was certain to be discovered during daylight. He closed his eyes in the darkness of the cocoon he'd made for himself and slept.

Carlos was exhausted. The brigade had had two days of heat and battle. The cool of night was soothing, but dusk brought the noseums out of the mangroves and swarms of mosquitoes from the Zapata swamps. The invasion had started well.   The battalions stormed ashore, established beachheads, and drove Castro's forces back. But the promised "umbrella" of air cover failed to materialize, and the attack had stalled. The few planes that did show up were coming from Nicaragua, 600 miles away. The brigade was nearly out of ammunition.

Morning dawned with incoming cannon and artillery fire. Carlos crouched at the bottom of his foxhole and covered his ears with his hands. The barrage intensified. Shells were exploding everywhere. The noise was deafening. Smoke burned his eyes and lungs. A shell landed nearby and knocked him senseless.

When he regained consciousness, he saw men from his unit moving back down the road toward Playa Giron. He picked up his rifle and followed them. He saw more shells exploding and men's lips moving but could hear nothing.

47

Diego sat in his living room, smoking, and fuming. Where could she have gone? A car squealed into the driveway. He heard boots running up the stone walkway followed by frantic knocking at the door. He tried to appear nonchalant as he walked to the door. He could allow no one to suspect the rage he was feeling. She would get what was coming to her soon enough. He opened the door and was surprised to see Colonel Gomez.

Gomez was sweating and agitated and carried a large manila envelope. He took in the relaxed attitude of Diego. "You haven't heard, have you?" he said.

"Heard what?"

"We're being invaded!"

"What? Invaded! Where?"

"In the east, near Santiago de Cuba!"

"I was just near there, yesterday," Diego said. "I heard nothing."

"It began early this morning." Gomez stopped to gauge the impact of his next revelation. "There's more," he said. He looked past Diego and scanned the room behind him.

"What do you mean, 'more'?" Diego said.

"Is your wife here?"

"Is my wife here? What difference could that possibly make to you? We're being invaded and you're asking me about my wife?"

"I've been given a list of people who are to be rounded up," Gomez said. "It has the names of subversives and spies who are suspected of working for the American CIA."

"Yes?" Diego said. "What does my wife have to do with your list? You're making me impatient, Colonel Gomez. Say what you have to say."

"Your wife is on it."

"My wife's on the list? You must be mistaken, Gomez. It can't be. That's completely crazy!"

"I didn't want to believe it either," Gomez said, "but I'm afraid it's true, *señor* Montalvo. She's been visiting a captain at the munitions depot and stealing explosives for the rebels. There are pictures."

"Pictures? What pictures?"

Gomez pulled some black and white photos from the envelope and handed them to Diego. "I'm sorry," he said.

Diego's mouth dropped. It couldn't be, but the pictures were unmistakable…it was Alyssa. He stumbled backwards until he reached his chair and fell into it. He shuffled through the photographs. "I can't believe it. Gomez, tell me this isn't true. My own wife, a spy?"

Gomez closed the door behind him and turned back to Diego. "It's true," he said. He nodded toward the stairway. "Is she here?"

Diego looked at him but seemed not to have heard Gomez's question. Gomez stepped in front of him and raised his voice. Diego Montalvo was his superior, but he was here on official business of the government. "Is your wife here!"

The volume of Gomez's question shook Diego back to his senses. He rose from the chair to his full height and looked down at his underling. Then the reality of the situation struck him. Cuba was under attack and his own wife had been photographed assisting the enemy. He sank back down. "No," he said. "I don't know where she is."

We must find her," Gomez said.

"Yes," Diego said. "She must be found."

Gomez raised his voice again. "No, *we* must find her, *señor*! El Commandante will not be happy when he finds out your wife is on this list. But, if *you* find her and bring her to justice, it may not go so badly for you."

Diego looked up at Gomez. The man was thinking clearly, and he was not. Castro would be angry, all right. Angry enough to have him shot. Diego rose again and put a hand on Gomez's shoulder.   He'd always despised Gomez for his conniving obsequiousness, but now Gomez was watching out for him. Diego began to feel a strange sort of kinship toward the man. *"Gracías, mi amigo,"* he said. "Thank you, Colonel Gomez. You're right. Let's go find her."

48

Still black with the soot he'd smeared on himself for the landing, unshaven, sweating and stripped to his waist, Magner sat exhausted in the communications room of the *Blagar.* In front of him was a microphone. All around the walls of the little room were speakers connecting him to the various areas of the battle, as well as to headquarters in Washington and the U.S. ships.

The situation on the beach continued to deteriorate. The messages coming into the *Blagar* from the 4th Battalion commander were getting more desperate. "Tanks closing on Blue Beach from north and east. They're firing directly at our headquarters."

Then, "Fighting on beach. Send all available aircraft, now!"

"In water, out of ammunition. Enemy closing in. Help must arrive in next hour."

And finally, "Am destroying all equipment and communications. I have nothing left to fight with. I'm taking to the woods."

An order came in to the *Blagar* from command headquarters in Washington. Magner and Ross and the remaining frogmen were to transfer to the naval destroyer *Eaton*. Reconnaissance planes had spotted survivors along the shore of Bahia de Cochinos. Their orders were to launch a rescue mission and bring them out.

They used lifeboat launches off the *Eaton* and rubber rafts to patrol the beaches of Bahia de Cochinos for survivors. Out in the bay, four American destroyers were anchored 1000 yards apart. Overhead, Air Force jets from the carrier *Essex* guarded the air while the rescue mission took place. The rescue boats flew big American flags to announce their presence to the survivors, but all was quiet. It seemed that most of the brigade's survivors had fled deep into the swamps. The first day of searching picked up only a dozen men. Among them was José. His arm was still in a tourniquet, and he was in obvious need of medical attention, but otherwise he was in reasonably good shape. Magner gave him a bear hug. "Where's Roberto?" he said.

José smiled. "He had some important business to attend to inland."

"Gotcha," Magner said. "Alyssa. I hope he wasn't planning to go through the swamps."

"He took the raft."

"Good. Let's get you out to the ship. That arm needs to be looked at."

"I wish you'd come to me when this happened," the ship's doctor said, when they were aboard the *Eaton*. "This doesn't look good. Your forearm's broken. I think I can save it, but it may never work exactly right again."

"Sorry, Doc," José said. "I was busy."

The Cuban soldiers were welcomed aboard the *Eaton* by the American sailors, who were upset, frustrated and nearly in tears. They cleaned the soldiers' weapons, gave them clean khakis, and insisted they eat at the captain's table. "Forgive us," an officer said to José. "Christ, I don't know what's going on in Washington. They fired on us, and we weren't allowed to fire back."

The following day, the rescue party went out again. It was hot. The beaches were scorching and forced the men to work in shifts. A search plane spotted a lone survivor. He sat under a mangrove tree and waved a stick with a white flag at the end of it. When Magner and the rescue team got closer, they saw another man lying on the ground next to the man with the stick. Wary of a trap, Ross's team moved in from the other side. The man continued to wave the flag back and forth. It was Carlos. He was wearing only his underwear. Many of the survivors were being found with their clothes shredded from the thorny bushes of the woods and swamps, or in some cases, totally naked. The man lying next to Carlos was dead. Magner lifted Carlos up in his arms and carried him like a baby back to the raft. A half hour later, they were in the medical room of the *Eaton*.

Carlos's lips were blistered and his throat was parched. He'd been drinking the brackish water in the swamps. José and Magner watched as the ship's doctor trickled fresh water down his throat. Drop by drop, the doctor dribbled the water in and massaged Carlos's throat to help him swallow. The doctor was able to get a pint of water into him and then another. Carlos tried to talk, but no sound came out. Finally, he was able to produce a low whisper. José leaned over him and put his ear near to Carlos's mouth. After a moment, José straightened and looked across the hospital bed at Magner.

"What'd he say?" Magner asked.

"He wants to know if we won."

49

When darkness fell, Roberto motored the raft west along the southern coast of Cuba. He estimated he had a little more than 100 kilometers to reach a spot on the southern coast directly opposite Havana on the north coast. There were two extra gas cans in the raft that he hoped would give him enough fuel to make it. From his landing point, he'd have another fifty kilometers of island to cross to get to Havana. The Isle of Pines, a large island almost due south of Havana, would appear on his left when it was time for him to make for shore.

He could still hear the engines of planes and patrol boats and wanted to stay in the seclusion of the mangroves near shore, but the mosquitoes were thick, so he moved further out from land to escape them. It was after midnight when he saw the lights of the Isle of Pines and turned up to the north.

The small community where he landed was dark. Roberto hot-wired a pickup truck and raced toward Havana. Halfway there, he stopped at a gasoline station that had closed for the night and used a pay phone to call his sister. It was two o'clock in the morning, but she answered on the first ring.

"Roberto," she said. "Thank God, it's you. Are you alright?"

"Yes, I'm fine, Maria. I have to find Alyssa."

"She's here," Maria said. "You must get her out of here, right away. The police are picking up everyone they suspect may have had a part in the invasion. I'm certain she's high on their list."

"Let me speak to her."

"Roberto," Alyssa said, when she got on the phone. "I knew it was you. Are you coming?"

"I'm coming now."

"It won't be safe for you to drive. They're stopping everyone who's on the roads."

"I'll get as close as I can and then come the rest of the way on foot. Do you know how we can get away?"

"It will be very difficult," Alyssa said. "Hundreds have been arrested.   Francisco and Jorge Fundora have both been killed. Castro is going crazy."

"Okay, we'll try to make it to the *Criollo*. What about your mother?"

"She's dead."

"I'm sorry," Roberto said. "And your father?"

"I don't know. I'll tell you all about it when we're out of here…hurry."

50

"We found her!" Gomez said. "She's at a house here in Havana."

Diego rose from behind his desk. He'd been going through the motions of trying to assist the counterattack efforts of the military but thinking always about Alyssa and racking his brain for where she might be hiding. "Alright," he said. "Let's go! We can't let her get away!" He grabbed his hat and ran with Gomez to the car.

Gomez drove recklessly through the city. The streets were nearly deserted with the army massed at the other end of the island. Residents were staying inside their homes, listening to reports of the battle on their radios. When they reached the house where Alyssa was reported to be staying, Diego held up a hand to Gomez. "Wait here," he said. "I'll handle this."

Alyssa hung up the phone and went to join Maria on the sofa in the darkened living room. Not wanting to attract attention, Maria had lit only a single candle. Alyssa was startled to find her holding a small pistol in the palm of her hand.

Maria saw the shock on Alyssa's face. "My husband gave it to me," she explained. "When he heard there was an invasion, he said I might need it. I don't need it, Alyssa. I want you to take it. *You* might need it."

"I don't think so," Alyssa said. "Besides, I've never even fired a gun. I wouldn't know what to do with it."

"That's what I said to my husband, but he insisted. He said that you just slide this little button up and pull the trigger."

Alyssa shook her head. "Guns frighten me," she said. "I don't think I could ever really shoot someone."

"I don't think I could either," Maria said. "If you don't want it, I'll put it back in the nightstand drawer." She stood and moved toward the bedroom. She'd taken only a few steps when the front door burst open. A tall man stepped into the dimly lit room. He exuded a bearing of self-importance and a sense of purpose in his movements.

Alyssa gasped. "Diego! What are you doing here?"

"I've been looking for *you*, my dear," Diego said. He took in the candlelit room. "Isn't this just cozy? Here you are with the sister of the man who deserted you." He turned to Maria who stood frozen in her tracks. "You're harboring a fugitive," he said. "My wife is a spy."

"No," Maria said.

"Oh yes," Diego said. "Her name's on a list of those who've been collaborating with the enemy. There are pictures."

Alyssa laughed. "There are no pictures," she said.

"There are," Diego said. "I've seen them. And what's worse is that Fidel will soon be seeing them, too. You've ruined me, Alyssa. You will certainly be shot, and I'll probably be shot, as well."

"You're mistaken," she said. "You're always getting things wrong, Diego. I'm being confused with someone else."

"I am *not* mistaken!" Diego said. "I know all about your clandestine meetings with Captain Rodriguez!"

"You know nothing," Alyssa said. Revulsion flushed through her. She no longer cared about hiding her contempt. Rising from the sofa, she took a step towards him. "You're a fool, Diego. You've always been a fool and you're still a fool."

"No," Diego said. "You may have cleverly deceived me, but I'm not a fool, Alyssa. We're defeating the Americans in spite of all your spying."

"Yes, you are a fool, Diego Montalvo. Isn't your willingness to believe that silly Sergeant Gomez and his preposterous tale about treasure proof enough of that?"

"Oh, but there is treasure," Diego said. He wagged a long finger at her and moved a step closer. "Your father admitted it to me."

"Liar!" Alyssa shouted. "If he told you that, it was only to get you to leave him alone." Her eyes narrowed as a terrible thought came to her. "Did you torture my poor father, Diego? You did, didn't you? Don't you know that could have killed him, you bastard!"

"I didn't kill him," Diego said. "He killed himself."

Alyssa stood stunned in the middle of the living room. "My father is dead?"

"Yes," Diego said. "He hung himself in his cell."

Alyssa imagined the scene behind these words and felt like collapsing, but her anger sustained her. "So, you've managed to kill both of my parents. I've never in my life hated anyone as much as I hate you, now. But even greater than my hate for you is my disgust. You're not a man, Diego, you're a filthy maggot, blindly crawling on your pale white belly through the putrid gutter of rot left by Castro."

A blow from the back of Diego's hand sent Alyssa flying across the room and back onto the sofa, where she lay sprawled. The clout was accompanied by the roar of a wounded beast and contained the sum of the rage that had been mounting within Diego since he'd seen the pictures. He was on top of her in an instant, his long fingers wrapped around her neck and his thumbs pressed hard against her windpipe. Alyssa tried to strike back but was pinned by his superior weight.

On the perimeter of the fog of his fury, Diego could hear a distant shouting. He heard it again and turned his head to discern the source. It took him a moment to realize that the dark hole he was staring into was the barrel of a small pistol. He released his hold on Alyssa and backed away.

"Get out of this house!" Maria shouted. She tried to sound threatening, but her voice came out shrill and trembling with fright.

Diego heard the fear in Maria's voice and smiled. "You won't shoot me," he said. "I'll leave your house, but my wife will be coming with me. She's a criminal and a traitor to her country."

Maria began to scream. She jumped up and down and stamped her feet in unison, like a petulant child. "Get out of here! Get out of here! Get out of here!"

Diego looked at her with surprise. This woman had gone insane. He took a step toward Maria to disarm her of the gun, but before he could reach her there was an explosive crack that echoed off the living room walls. In the semi-darkness, a quick tongue of fire darted from the barrel of the pistol.

The shock of the gun's report made Maria stop jumping. She and Alyssa stared at the small black hole that appeared in Diego's white shirtfront. A red stain began to seep into the fabric around the hole. Diego looked down at his chest, then up at Maria and then over to where Alyssa still lay on the sofa, an appeal for mercy in his eyes.

Alyssa's eyes met his. This was the man who'd taken her family's home, destroyed her parents, kept her from leaving the country with the man she loved and manipulated her into marrying him. She said nothing, but her unfeeling expression communicated that she thought he deserved nothing less. Diego's legs weakened. He fought to stay upright, but his tall figure began to shorten. He collapsed downward onto his knees, as though melting into himself, and then pitched face forward onto the floor – still and lifeless.

It was another hour before Roberto entered quietly in through the back of the house, dirty and exhausted. He wrapped Alyssa and Maria in long embraces. In the living room, Diego's corpse still lay where it had fallen, the gun by its side. Roberto displayed neither surprise nor remorse when he recognized the dead man. "Who shot him?"

"I did," Maria said. "It was an accident."

Roberto picked up the gun and wiped it with the tail of his shirt to remove Maria's fingerprints. Then he squeezed the grip to leave his own fingerprints on its surface and dropped it next to Diego's body. "Okay," he said to Maria. "Give us a couple hours and then alert the authorities. Tell them Diego and I fought, and I shot him."

51

Roberto and Alyssa slipped out of the house and began to thread their way through Havana under the shadows of the night. The man who'd been watching Maria's house from across the street stepped from his car and began to follow them.

Alyssa's emotions were running at a high pitch. The thrill of being with Roberto was tempered by her fear of being caught. The tragic deaths of her parents weighed heavily on her heart.

Neither of them spoke, but relief and longing caused them to take every opportunity to make physical contact with the other. All was quiet when they reached the Naval Academy. Roberto stole aboard *Criollo* and rapped at the door of the captain's cabin.

A sleepy, but familiar voice growled from the interior. "Who's there?"

"It's me, Roberto."

Oliva opened the cabin door and embraced Roberto. "So, you're still alive, eh? Good."

"*Sí,*" Roberto said, "but we must leave Cuba as soon as possible."

His encompassing "we" alerted Oliva to the presence of Alyssa, standing in the darkness of the main cabin. "Oh," he said.

"This is Alyssa," Roberto said. "She's José's cousin."

"*Con mucho gusto, señorita*," Oliva said. "She's very beautiful, Roberto."

"Yes," Roberto said, "she is. Unfortunately, I think both of us have overstayed our welcome in this country. The authorities will soon be looking for us."

"Take *Criollo*."

"Are you sure?" Roberto said. "Do you want to go with us?"

"No, my friend, I'll go to live with my sister. *Criollo* has been my life, but I'm tired. She's been waiting for you…now she can be *your* lives. Take good care of her, but hurry, the tide is on its way out. If I give you a good push-off, you can float out of the harbor with the tide and not have to start the engine or put up the sails. With luck, you'll not be noticed."

Roberto embraced Oliva. "*Muchas gracias*, old friend."

Alyssa hugged him, also. "I'm glad to have finally met you, Oliva. I've heard so much about you from Roberto and José."

Oliva smiled. "It's been my great pleasure, s*eñorita.*"

They rushed to untie the boat and leaped aboard. Oliva wrapped his arms around a piling and gave them a final shove away from the dock with one strong kick of his leg. "*Vaya con Dios, mi amigos.*"

Alyssa blew him a silent kiss. Then her eyes widened. Before she could shout a warning, Oliva was struck down from behind by the butt of Gomez's pistol. Gomez walked to the end of the dock and leveled the gun at Alyssa. The boat had drifted out too far for him to jump to it, but it was still only a few feet away and it would be an easy shot. "Tell me, where the treasure is, *señor*, or I'll shoot her," he said to Roberto, not taking his eyes from Alyssa.

Roberto left the wheel and stepped toward Alyssa.

"Stay away from her," Gomez said.

Roberto stopped.

"Tell me quickly, *señor*, or you'll soon have a dead girlfriend. That would be a shame. She's so pretty."

Roberto's mind was racing. He could think of nothing to say or do that could save them. They were easy targets. Gomez's hand clenched once, and the crack of his pistol split the night. Roberto and Alyssa heard the whiz of a bullet pass close above their heads.

"I have no more patience, *señor*," Gomez said. Again, he aimed the pistol at Alyssa. "The next one will not be a warning."

A swift movement came from behind Gomez. There was a blur of something being wrapped around his neck. It was Oliva. He'd looped a dock line around Gomez's neck and was pulling it tight. The muscles of his forearms bulged with the effort.

Gomez's neck stretched backward. Panic filled his eyes. He stared skyward, his eyes protruding grotesquely from the pressure of the thick line crushing his windpipe. The gun dropped from his hand and his tongue searched the night air for oxygen.

When his gurgling stopped, Oliva let him fall forward into the water. He stood at the end of the dock a few moments and watched the body sink down into the inky blackness of the lagoon. Then, he shrugged his shoulders and disappeared into the night.

52

Criollo floated silently with the outgoing tide down through the harbor, past El Morro, and out through the harbor entrance. It wasn't until she was in the open ocean that Roberto raised the sails and pointed her westward.

Alyssa hugged him from behind. "Where're we going?" she said.

"Isla Paraiso."

"Isla Paraiso." Alyssa rolled the words around her tongue. "It sounds so nice and I'm so tired, Roberto."

"Lie down and get some sleep. I can handle the boat and we'll be there in a few short hours. The end of all this madness is in sight."

The wind was fresh, *Criollo* raced before it at twelve knots. They were well off the coast by daybreak and sighted Isla Paraiso by noon. Roberto dropped the sails and started the engine. They wound their way through the narrow channel to the dock on the south side of the little island. The dock was too small for *Criollo*, so Roberto dropped an anchor off the bow and brought the stern around to the dock. Paco came down when he heard the chugging of the boat's diesel. He caught the stern lines when they were thrown to him and tied them around the two big pilings at each end of the dock.

Roberto stepped off the fantail of *Criollo* onto the dock to an enthusiastic greeting from Paco. "Roberto," Paco said, "we knew you'd come back someday. Lena! Lena!" he called. "Come see who's here!"

Lena hurried down the path, brushing the dirt from her hands on the apron she used for gardening. "Roberto, Roberto!" she said when she saw him. Her eyes filled with tears. *"Bienvenido*, Roberto, welcome back to Paraiso!"

Roberto introduced Alyssa and explained their situation. "You'll be safe here," Paco said. "No one ever comes here, and your boat is hidden from the sea on this side of the island. From here, it's all reefs for miles. No one can come within sight of this side."

Paco and Lena shared Isla Paraiso with an old couple that lived on the north side of the island. The old couple had seen the big sailboat come in the channel and came over to satisfy their curiosity. Lena introduced them to Roberto and Alyssa. "We can't tell anyone that they're here."

"Why not?" the old woman asked.

"Castro's looking for them. We must keep their being here a secret."

The woman gave them a look of suspicion.

"Welcome to our island," the old man said. "We'll tell no one." He put a finger to his lips and gave them a conspiratorial smile.

"Thank you," Roberto said. "We must sleep now. We're both exhausted."

"Yes," Paco said. "Sleep, sleep. We'll not wake you."

"When you wake up, I'll have plenty for you to eat," Lena said.

"You should call the authorities," the old lady said to her husband when they returned to their side of the island.

"Why should I call the authorities?" the old man said.

"They'll get us all in trouble. If you don't tell the authorities and they're discovered here, there will be trouble for all of us. Besides, there's probably a reward for turning them in."

"To do such a thing would be unforgivable. They're nice young people who've done nothing to us. Whatever they're running from, we'd probably run from, too. And don't forget, they're Lena and Paco's friends. What a despicable idea." He turned away.

"If you don't call the authorities, I will," the old lady said to her husband's back. "You can go to jail if you want, but I'm *not*. And, if there's a reward, I'd be a fool not to get it."

The old man turned back to her – his face a dark cloud. He took a step towards her and shook his forefinger. "Don't you dare say a word about this to *anyone*! Do you hear me? Not a *word*!"

Roberto and Alyssa were having breakfast ashore with Paco and Lena. Bahia de Cochinos seemed a world away, but the feelings of tranquility they were experiencing were foreign to them. They'd become used to lives of turmoil. The peace of Isla Paraiso was hard to trust. As the need to be on guard dissipated, their fear and dread lifted and the fullness of their feelings for each other surged to take their place. They indulged themselves in loving looks and touches, and dreams for the future.

A shout came from the other side of the island. "You stupid, stupid, woman!" The old man came running over the hill. "She's done it, she's done it! She radioed the authorities that you're here. She thought she'd get a reward. I'm sorry, I'm so sorry."

Stunned, they sat back from their breakfasts…the other shoe had dropped. Paco shook his head in disgust and pushed away from the table. "You'd better get going," he said.

Roberto sighed…so much for peace. "We'd better."

They hurried to gather themselves and raced down to the boat. Roberto leaped aboard and started the engine. If they could get *Criollo* beyond the twelve-mile limit before the patrol boats caught up with them, they might be safe. The patrols were unlikely to follow them into international waters. Paco and Lena threw off the dock lines. Roberto wheeled *Criollo* into the channel and gunned the engine.

He had the sails up before they left the channel and fell off toward the west when they passed beyond the marker buoy. He set *Criollo* on a broad reach and lashed the wheel. Then he pulled out the boat's binoculars and scanned the sea behind them…nothing. Maybe the authorities hadn't believed the old woman. Maybe Castro had bigger fish to catch. But the next time he looked, he saw a small black speck come into view over the horizon and continue to grow larger by the minute.

"What can we do?" Alyssa said.

"Nothing," Roberto said. "It's a Russian-made patrol boat that can do forty knots an hour. That's three times faster than we're going. They'll be on top of us in twenty minutes."

53

Magner, José and Carlos were in the officers' mess aboard the destroyer Eaton, finishing their breakfasts, when they were approached by the ship's chief communications officer. "How you guys doing?"

"Not bad, considering," Magner said.

"Well, if you want something to do and you think you're up to it, we could use your help down in the communications room. We're intercepting a lot of Cuban radio messages. Our boys can't keep up. We were hoping you might be able to help translate."

"Sure thing," Magner said.

"I'll go with you," José said.

"You guys go ahead," Carlos said. "My head's still too scrambled for me to be much use.".

"Go back to bed," Magner said. "We've got this."

They were given seats at a small metal table in the communications room. Each of them was issued a tape recorder and a stack of tapes. "Listen to some of these, will you?" the chief communications officer said. "See if you can get a read on any of them. I think the skipper just wants to make sure that we get out of here without starting World War III. If you guys get anything interesting, give me a heads up. Good luck."

Magner and José put on their headphones and began listening to messages between Cuban military units that had been intercepted over the last several days. Most of them were self-congratulations for having defeated the Americans.

They'd been at their job for several hours without hearing anything important when the communications officer came over with another tape. "This one just came in," he said. "Have a listen and see what you think. It sounds like something interesting may be happening just a few miles up ahead of us."

Magner put the tape in his recorder. "Sounds like an excited old woman," he said across the table to José. "She lives on an island and she's telling the authorities back in Cuba about someone trying to escape in a sailboat."

"Let me listen to it, it could be Roberto and Alyssa in the *Criollo*." Magner passed José the headphones. He listened a minute and smiled. "It's them all right, but it sounds like they're about to have one of Castro's patrol boats hot on their tail."

"Hey," Magner called across the room to the communications officer, "we've got something. Get a message up to the skipper right away!"

Alyssa looked back at the menacing black speck, crashing through the ocean, and growing larger by the minute. She turned to Roberto. "Come, my love. Lie with me one last time." She removed her clothing and stretched out on the port cushion of the cockpit.

Roberto watched. She was beautiful, lying naked in the sun…calm and confident with the end only minutes away. He dropped his own clothes to the deck and joined her.

When the sound of the patrol boat's engine reached them, they remained entwined in the cockpit of *Criollo* – lost in their embrace. In moments they'd be captured, taken back to Havana, and sent before a firing squad. Suddenly, all went silent. The roar of the patrol boat's motor stopped. The warmth of the morning sun was blocked out and *Criollo* was plunged into the cool of a massive shadow.

Roberto and Alyssa raised themselves up from their lovemaking and peered over the rail. A towering gray wall had materialized next to them. It took a moment to realize it was the steel hull of an American destroyer. Familiar voices called down to them from the deck high above. It was José with his arm in a sling,

Chip Magner and Carlos. The destroyer halted between *Criollo* and the Cuban patrol boat.

Up in the wheelhouse of the destroyer, the skipper sipped his coffee and smiled down upon the angry, gesticulating band of men on Castro's patrol boat. "If we can do nothing else," he said to the helmsman, "at least we can do this."

Roberto jumped into his shorts and unlashed the wheel. He swung the boat around while Alyssa wrapped herself in his shirt. He pulled the *Criollo* up next to the destroyer. "The cavalry arrives! I thought it was all over for us!"

"We intercepted a message from Isla Paraiso about two people escaping on a sailboat!" José said. "I knew it had to be you!"

"How's your arm?" Alyssa said.

José waved his cast around. "Okay," he said. "I've still got it, anyway."

"Where are you two headed?"

Roberto swept his arm across the horizon in front of them. "Somewhere out there! I'll write to my father when we reach land and let everyone know where we are!"

"Do you need money?" Magner asked.

Roberto shook his head and pointed down at the hull of the sailboat. "Thanks, but I think we'll be fine!"

Jose smiled. "They've got the rest of the treasure down in the keel," he said to Magner.

"You'd better hurry up and get beyond the twelve-mile limit!" Magner shouted. "The patrols on the other side don't look happy."

Roberto turned the sailboat back toward the west and re-lashed the wheel. He and Alyssa stood together on the fantail and waved. *Criollo* sailed away, distancing herself further and further from the destroyer and the Cuban patrol boat.

Alyssa put her arm around Roberto and buried her head in his neck. "Where *are* we going, my darling?"

"How does Costa Rica sound? It should be out ahead of us somewhere."

"It sounds fine…I guess I don't really care as long as we're together. Say, what did you mean when Magner asked if we had any money and you pointed to the boat? Are you planning to sell it?"

Roberto smiled. "No, it's just that we happen to be transporting a small fortune in emeralds."

Alyssa stepped back. "Roberto, you're not serious. Are you telling me that crazy story about treasure is actually true?"

"Every word of it. As incredible as it sounds, it's all true. Maria, Tomo and I found the map. My father figured out where the treasure was buried, and your father safeguarded it. When he knew he was going to be arrested, he gave it to José and me to hide. We used a lot of it to supply the rebels and outfit the brigade, but the old chest is still down there in the keel and half-full of emeralds."

Alyssa shook her head and laughed. "I can't believe it. I really can't believe it...that's amazing!" She laid a hand on Roberto's shoulder. "So, we can try to free Cuba, again?"

"Yes, and next time we'll finish the job."

"Okay, someday, but not now. Now, we have something else to finish. Where were we, my love?" She lay back on the port cushion and opened her arms to him. "I think I was here…and you were...here."

THE END

AFTERWORD

The primary resource and inspiration for this novel is based upon the early life experiences of Dr. Enrique Rivera. Enrique and I first met in 1991 in Wellington, Florida. We were both psychologists and soon after our initial meeting, I joined his practice at Wellington Psychological Associates. We have remained good friends as have our wives, who are both gourmet cooks. After a few mojitos, a fine meal and a loud game of cubilete, we have often discussed the events of his youth over Grand Marnier and cigars late into the evening.

Enrique is from Santa Fe, Cuba, where his father rolled cigars, most notably Winston Churchill's figurados. He was still a boy when a lead pipe with a cross on its side, containing an old treasure map, was discovered near his home. The pipe was confiscated by Batista's repressive government, never to be seen again. The area was cordoned off and bulldozers began excavating. When he was eighteen, Enrique passed the rigorous qualifying examinations to become a cadet at the Cuban Naval Academy where he sailed in the St. Pete/Havana yacht race aboard the Criollo. When the tyranny of Fidel Castro became apparent, Enrique escaped via Puerto Rico to the U.S. His father left soon after in his old boat. After running out of gas, he was found drifting in the Gulfstream by a British freighter.

The story about the prison farm, the boy with the cookie and the harrowing escape at night to Guantanamo on beach rafts is a personal saga of courage and desperation shared with me by Juan Tomé, a restauranteur in North Palm Beach. His daughter, Alyssa, has a son whom she named Cristobal.

On New Year's Day, 1959, as Fidel Castro marched on Havana, Fulgencio Batista fled Cuba for the Dominican Republic with an estimated $300,000,000.

(Cover art by Lauren Walsh of Mackinac Island, Michigan)

www.ingramcontent.com/pod-product-compliance
Lightning Source LLC
Chambersburg PA
CBHW071242300726
48975CB00002B/530